YELLOW BEAR
——— *and* ———
SILVER SHOES

BUDDY JOHNSON

authorHOUSE®

AuthorHouse™
1663 Liberty Drive
Bloomington, IN 47403
www.authorhouse.com
Phone: 1 (800) 839-8640

Published by AuthorHouse 10/17/2017

ISBN: 978-1-5462-1042-9 (sc)
ISBN: 978-1-5462-1041-2 (e)

YELLOW BEAR
———— AND ————
SILVER SHOES

Atop the Unaka Mountain overlooking the many ridges and valleys, looking out across the vast expanse from east to west I became aware of distant mountains that my father could name without a moment's hesitation and point out the lay of the *"Old Trace the Old Wagon Road."*

Years upon years ago many events occurred and some of them were formed into stories that were told to children around the campfire when they camped along the "Old Trails."

As time changed the children into old men, a few stories were told over and over until they became woven into the fabric of folklore.

Now, I cannot name but a few of the mountains, my father is gone… no doubt most of the "Indian Tales" are gone too, lost in the pages of time. Aided with folklore and imagination, maybe we can unweave one or two stories that otherwise might have been lost.

When I was but a lad, many was the "Old Stories" I heard and one of those was most fascinating, the story of a lost mine, "Lost Treasure of Long Ago," and another was one called "Bear Wallow," a little flat at the head of a long valley where bears were seen that were eerie looking because of the yellow mud holes that they wallowed in.

Perhaps the story of Yellow Bear and his horse that wore silver shoes is one of those tales that has been uncovered from the lost pages of time.

BUDDY JOHNSON

The date was October 26, 1843. Jake Cooper, a lonely old man, and his grandson John had set up their hunting camp in one of the dark hollows of the Unaka Mountain. The weather was bad and looking like it might snow. This was John's first hunting trip with his grandfather. He was in hopes the weather would hold because this trip would be Jake's last hunting trip of the year. John was hoping to hunt for two weeks. After the fourth day they setttled down by the campfire to reflect on the past day of hunting

The old man's luck hadn't been very good and jokingly he asked John to borrow his good luck charm. John had a large silver coin that he sometimes carried. About five years ago he'd found the coin in a bank of the Red Fork Creek. No one had been able to identify it and the only thing anyone could make out on the coin was the date; 1547, but they all agreed it was pure silver.

Jake said, "John, there's a legend of a silver mine somewhere in the Unaka and possibly your coin is one that has been made from silver right here on the Unaka Mountain."

"Grandpaw, do you know about the lost mine?" John asked.

"Yes John, I've heard some tales about the silver mine. When I was about your age, an old Indian told me about the mine. My mother was his sister."

"He was your uncle? Are you Cherokee? What was his name?" John asked

"The old Indian's name was Nashayeool. But when he was a young warrior they called him Yellow Bear; and yes John, I'm Cherokee Indian."

"If you are Indian, that means I'm part Indian too."

"Yes John, your Mother is Cherokee Indian."

"Grandpaw, how come? What did you say his name was? Yellow Bear, well how come he has two names?"

The old man was tired and sleepy. He didn't want to talk half of the night, but he said, "Yellow Bear was the name the Chief of his tribe had given him when he was born. When he was about ten or eleven he'd been out hunting for the men that was his enemy. One of them had shot a hole through his left ear. When he returned to the tribe they called him Nashayeool, which meant brave with a hole in one ear. Now let's get some sleep and tomorrow I'll tell you about the Indian boy."

John laid there thinking about the old Indian with two names. He began to wonder, *what year was it when yellow Bear was eleven years old.* Thinking about how things were back then and wondering why Yellow Bear, an Indian boy eleven years old, had enemies that were trying to kill him. As John drifted off to sleep a vision appeared. He could see a long valley, a huddled village of wigwams where a tribe of Indians was camped. In the center of the village a meeting was going on. This was the beginning of a tribal council. He could see the Chief, two elders and two medicine men. The elder medicine man turned toward John hesitating just for a moment. The old medicine man looked familiar; he looked like Jake Cooper, John's grandfather. He knew he must satisfy his curiosity and he stepped closer, stepping between the rows of wigwams. With the silence of a cat, he was almost ready to step into the council when he was waked up by cold snow blowing in his face. Jake was already up and packing the hides, furs and meat. When he saw that John was awake, he told him to grab a bite or two and get ready to head for home because there was an early snow storm blowing in. John noticed the strong wind lashing through the camp and Jake's pack horse was acting nervous. John said he could wait until they got home to eat, so he went to the horse to calm him while Jake tied the stuff on and then they headed down the dark hollow towards Jake's. By the time they got there, the snow had already covered the trail and was still coming down in big heavy waves. Jake knew it would be most difficult for John to make it home before dark because it was five miles or more and the snow would be waist deep by then. So, John would have to stay with him until the storm broke. They put Jake's horse in one end of the shed that was attached to the back of his log cabin and put the meat and hides in the other end. It was nearly noon but still dark inside because of the storm. Jake built a fire in the fireplace and sat down in his chair. John sat on the stool on the other side and waited for the fire to catch up and light the room.

"Grandpaw, I'm hungry," John said.

"Me too. While the fire catches up let's cut into some of that venison we just brought in. With some potatoes, peppers and onions I'll make us a big pot of stew."

Jake's wife had died many years ago and he'd learned to do his own cooking. The old man sure knew how to make a tasty pot of stewed venison. Today's stew was as good as John had ever tasted. After both of them had all of the stew they wanted, Jake said, "John, why don't you put some potatoes in the coals to roast; I think it's going to be a long night."

John went into the other room and came back with both hands full of potatoes. He dug out a hole in the fire coals and was about finished when he remembered this morning and his dream of this medicine man that looked like his grandpaw.

"Grandpaw, did you ever live with the Indians?" John asked.

"I spent some time with Nashayeool. He stayed with me and your grandmother four or five years, his voice trailed off."

"Did he ever tell you any tales or Indian stories other than the one about the lost mine?"

"Yes John, the old Indian spoke many tales of the Cherokee. He told one story that I was real fond of. It was a story about his grandfather; a medicine man named Black Raven. John, if you will carry in enough firewood to last the night, I'll tell you the story of Yellow Bear and a horse that wore silver shoes."

"Wow!", John said, and hurried to carry in the fire wood.

"John, when the old Indian came to live with us it was in the winter, sixty some years ago." Then thinking for a minute he continued, "I don't know if they were Spaniards or not, but he spoke of them as; 'The men in iron hats'. The story sticks in my mind like mud does to my buckskin boots. We would sit on the grass mats in our one room cabin and he would tell me this story of a medicine man, a great wizard, and how he revealed to him the mysteries of life. He began the story by saying, Yellow Bear or Nashayeool, as he was later known, was a nosy ten-year old Indian, always asking questions and following in Black Raven's footsteps. There was a place on the western side of the Unaka Mountain, a place called Bear Wallow. There was yellow mud holes there where the bears would wallow in them until they were yellow. He was born there and that was why he had the name Yellow Bear."

"The place was thought to be sacred ground; a place to hold councils and carry on with important talks. Yellow Bear was always nosing around and listening in on the council meetings."

John could almost envision, a big council meeting. With memories of stories that had been told many years ago, Jake spoke in the manner of an old Indian story teller.

"Yellow Bear, what do you think you are up to?" asked Black Raven.

"I want to hear what's being said."

"Your nosing around where you're not supposed to be is going to get you in trouble. You know you're not to hear what's said at the meeting of medicine men. Only the wise speak at the council talks."

"Grandfather, you're wise. Why aren't you speaking?"

"I don't want to speak, not yet. Tonight I'm like the Yellow Bear, just want to listen."

"But grandfather, you sit on all councils. Why not this one?"

"Yellow Bear, I'm not in favor of trading silver mines for muskets, iron pots and furs."

"Why not Grandfather?"

"I don't trust men who wear iron hats. They are in big hurry."

"Why do they hurry Grandfather?"

"Yellow Bear, I fail to know. I shook medicine bones four times. Four times they don't tell good or bad about strange men. So I don't sit and talk."

"Grandfather, might something go wrong with trade? Is that the reason?"

"Yellow Bear, only one time medicine bones not give me a sign, and that time we lost many braves in battle at Big Sandy River."

Yellow Bear could tell by the broken words that he was troubled by the men in iron hats.

"Grandfather, why not talk more about trade and make time for spirits over medicine bones to answer?"

"Yellow Bear, you give me good thoughts for next council. Tomorrow night I'll set and talk trade and someday you will sit at my side at councils of medicine men."

"Grandfather, how many councils until trade is sealed?"

"Five more. Then we smoke pipe and make final bargain."

"Grandfather, this silver mine, what if men in iron hats don't know big mine from little mine?"

"Yellow Bear, there is only one big mine."

Grandfather, why not take silver from big mine and make little mine to see if men who wear iron hats satisfy easily? Would not that give spirits time to speak?"

"Yellow Bear, your words are wise beyond your age. Tomorrow you and I will get help and make false mine. Then I will set on council and speak, because a plan has taken shape in my mind."

He would take some silver from the mine and bury it in the floor of a cave that he knew of and to make it appear more real, he'd drive some pieces into the cracks and crevices of the walls. If that trade was good for the tribe, he'd speak in favor of the real mine.

Long before daybreak, Black Raven, Yellow Bear and two chosen braves were in the mine working out pieces and chunks of silver. By sundown they had the cave made to look like a real mine.

That night at the second meeting of council members, it was Black Ravens turn to speak first. He told the Chief, the Elders and White Wolf, the other medicine man of the tribe, that he thought something was wrong with the trade and requested more time to pass before the final bargain.

"How much time?" the Chief asked.

"Another full moon, maybe two should pass."

The Chief and two Elders agreed that the request of Black Raven was wise, but White Wolf reminded them that the men in iron hats were in a hurry and the tribe would lose out if the trade went bad.

When it came Black Raven's turn to speak, he said, "If men in iron hats only want silver to trade with others, surely they will wait one moon. I look back at first council of trade. Their leader said that they want to get silver and return to their homeland. Has anyone asked how they move such a vast amount to the sea where ships wait? Is two moons too much to ask?"

White Wolf spoke, "Maybe men in iron hats have many more men to help move silver to the sea."

Black Raven then asked, "What if the men in iron hats have many men and outnumber our braves? Would that not put us at a disadvantage if they did not keep their promise? They could take our silver and leave us without silver or muskets. After we make trade would not that put us at loss for silver to bargain with? More than one time we should have silver to bargain with."

White Wolf spoke, "All of tribe will be better after trade. We will have fine muskets and iron pots to last many seasons. We must make trade before men in iron hats go away."

Black Raven started to speak but gave his turn to one of the Elders. He was thinking that maybe White Wolf was favoring the strange men over his own tribe. *Would White Wolf betray the tribe?*

Most of the next day Black Raven was busy putting his thoughts together for the council so his words would be understood by each one. It bothered him that his medicine bones did not give a sign, and was troubled by White Wolf's haste. All of Black Raven's life he had been taught that what one knew he kept to himself to better his own wisdom and knowledge.

The Chief started the third council with his usual chant then the youngest council member started the talk with his desire for one of the many muskets that the men in iron hats wanted to trade for silver. When it came Black Raven's turn to speak, he said, "At this council I speak for two, Yellow Bear and me. Yellow Bear speaks words of a sage. First my words, 'Is this trade good or bad for our tribe?' Neither way can I speak at this council. I should have answer in two moons. Yellow Bear speaks words of a sage. A false mine to trade men in iron hats to learn if they satisfy easily."

The Chief spoke, "If trade not be good for tribe, we should not trade silver."

White Wolf spoke, "We do not know that and what words of wisdom does a ten-year old have to speak? What does Yellow Bear have to speak about?"

8

Black Raven spoke, "The Cherokee have many ways to learn wisdom. By day and by night, when day passes and night comes, when darkness falls upon one that travels in a strange land he cannot clearly see which way the trail winds. When one doesn't know what pitfall might lie ahead, the wise would wait until the next light. Only the fool hearted travel the dark trails of strange lands when he can't see. Are not the men in iron hats strange men with strange ways?"

White Wolf raised his hand and then spoke, "Do we not appear strange to them? We hunt in the forest with sticks that bend and cast sticks tipped with stone that we call arrows. Do we not cover our flesh with skins and furs that once covered the animals? Is that not common to us?"

Black Raven spoke, "Before the men in iron hats came to our land, we did not know there were others that differ in ways from ours. All tribes of our land use hides and furs of the animal. This has been the way of our existence and the existence of all our forefathers. The medicine men that sat in these councils long before us, they did not know of these things that confront and confound us. They had no knowledge. They had no questions. They required no answers. They taught us their ways of medicine. If we fail to use that knowledge we will have failed the teaching of the wise ones. If we fail to make wise decisions, then all of our tribe will suffer from our ills."

White Wolf raised his hand, "I fail to vision how any one of our tribe could suffer any ill from the trade. Must I remind Black Raven that it will not be long until the chill winds of winter comes to the valleys and the Indian will have to hunt in the forest with his bow and arrow to feed and cover the bodies of our tribe? Will the silver help fill Black Raven's stomach or warm his body when it still lays buried deep inside the Unaka?"

Black Raven started to speak, but the Chief raised both hands signaling the end of this meeting. Black Raven was offended by the

Chief ending the council. No doubt the Chief was now in favor of White Wolf's words. Black Raven was now at risk of losing his turn at the council. If the Chief signaled two more councils to end, Black Raven would have to give up his seat at the council. Then White Wolf would be the elder medicine man.

Black Raven pondered the situation throughout the next day. He hardly paid any attention to Yellow Bear even when he asked about the little mine. The words of Yellow Bear about a false mine was what brought ill feeling towards Black Raven. Yet he somehow knew Yellow Bear's words were wise, but now he must be extra careful at tonight's council. Tonight he must choose his words with the wisdom of a true medicine man.

The third council was started with the usual chant. Normally he would have given the elder permission to start the council meeting, but he motioned to White Wolf to speak. White Wolf turned to face Black Raven and said, "Does Black Raven have sage words to speak; or does he carry words of Yellow Bear, the ten-year old that follows his grandfather like a shadow follows the man at mid-morning of summer?"

The Chief raised his right hand in protest of White Wolf's words and spoke, "It will be ten years before Yellow Bear can speak at a council. I find wisdom in Black Raven carrying the words of Yellow Bear to the council. Though Yellow Bear is not allowed to speak for himself, did he ask with wonder, if the men in iron hats would satisfy easily? Who has thought to ask this question? Are his words not worthy of a test? Three councils have passed without one asking:, 'how many muskets and iron knives can we get in trade for part of silver mine?' Would it satisfy us if we get the number of muskets we want?"

It was now White Wolf's turn to speak, and he said, "Men in iron hats want all of the silver. They will not trade for less." Then it was Black Ravens turn to speak, and he asked, "Has White Wolf spoken with men in iron hats of his own desire outside of our council? Did his words tell about the size of our mine? Did White Wolf describe what our mine is like from the inside? Do the strange men know of these things?"

The Chief raised his left hand and said, "Two more meetings then men in iron hats will sit at our council and bargain for final time and smoke pipe." It does seem that White Wolf would hurry without a test of Yellow Bear's words. Then he signaled to White Wolf to speak. White Wolf questioned, "How does Black Raven test the wisdom of one so young. Does he use words of Yellow Bear to satisfy his own thoughts and desires?"

Black Raven responded, "When words of wisdom are spoken, do they have to come from one that is old? It is my desire for White Wolf to sit and smoke pipe with men in iron hats and bargain for fine muskets, knives, iron pots and furs with stripes that are strange. I ask for two moons to pass, if they do not pass before final council. I request that Yellow Bears words be tested, but only after I decide."

White Wolf spoke, "How are sage words of Yellow Bear to have meaning? I fail to see how they could be words of wisdom."

The Chief spoke, "Black Raven, is there something I am not understanding? Am I failing to vision something out of order, after the trade? When do we test the wisdom of Yellow Bear? You were chosen as the senior medicine man because of your wisdom, your knowledge that was gained from battles. If I fail to have answers, I must end this council."

Black Raven spoke, "I have set on the council of many talks. I have led many braves into battle against the enemy. Have we not won seventeen of the twenty battles that I have led? I harbor great fear of battle with men in iron hats. Our arrows and great spears would have little affect against their armor. Do they have knowledge over many other things and ways that we have no understanding of? Of that I am certain, yet I have no proof nor do I have any evidence. I do have a cave with chunks of silver buried in the floor and in the walls to trade with men in iron hats for muskets to use against them if need be. If trade was to go bad, would it not be satisfying to know that strange men do not have all of the Cherokee silver?"

White Wolf spoke, "Is Black Raven and his make believe mine not more deceitful than our worst enemy? Does he desire to deceive those that have come to bargain and trade with us? Did these strange men come here to do us harm? Do they not bring things to trade for what we have no need of? Will they not go to the north where other tribes will be willing to trade? We have no great need of the silver that lies buried in the Unaka no matter how vast the amount. Does it matter to Black Raven how many horse loads the Unaka mine may contain?"

The Chief raised his right hand in protest of White Wolf's words. "I see great wisdom in the words that Yellow Bear has spoken to Black Raven. Does one know how many horse loads it will require to remove the entire amount of silver from the mine of the Unaka? This question I ask of White Wolf."

White Wolf said, "To answer that, one must know many things. Does not a different horse carry a different load? Do not the ladings be of different size?"

The Chief knew that White Wolf could not answer his first question, he asked more. "White Wolf, he asked, Do men in iron hats hurry?" Do they insist that we hurry so that in our haste we might fail to ask questions of wisdom at our council?"

Knowing that he could not answer, he got up and walked away from the council. Black Raven then had reason to believe he did favor the men in iron hats.

The Chief continued, "Tomorrow we will move more silver into the cave of Black Raven. Then I can speak to their leader that we have dug out much silver and wait for trade." He motioned to Black Raven, "Yellow Bear has spoken words of wisdom and should be rewarded. Does Black Raven have any words of reward for Yellow Bear?"

Black Raven thought; many years ago--when a young brave--I had spoken powerful words and was rewarded with four medicine sticks from the elder medicine man.

"Does Black Raven have something befitting for one so young?"

"I have. Those I have possessed since Yellow Bear's grandmother was a beautiful young maiden." He hadn't thought of them in many years and memories of the old medicine sticks carried his mind back to the time he was a young brave; when his father, Red Cloud was Chief, White Sage, his mother and Little Fox was Black Raven's son; the father of Yellow Bear who had been killed in the raid of another tribe. He was almost certain that Yellow Bear was listening in on the council. He said, "Long ears catch words like rain in gulley. I'll go get Yellow Bear, but first I get medicine sticks."

Shortly he returned to the council without the sticks or Yellow Bear.

"Can't find Yellow Bear, but tomorrow night I'll have words for him and make present to him with medicine sticks." He hadn't gone after the medicine sticks because fond memories had clouded his mind. He knew he'd have to put memories of sorrowed times behind him and think on words to speak at tomorrow night's council.

The fourth council was started with the usual chant, then the young council member started the meeting and then came Black Raven's turn. Today he had given much thought about many things, but he would speak first of his desires.

"Today we have moved much silver. Our desires are not to deceive anyone. We desire to learn the ways of these strange men who wear strange coverings over their bodies. We desire that the red man may own iron pots and cook our food like the white man. We desire the knowledge of trade. The knowledge of values and values of the Cherokee's possessions that we might bargain with wisdom of value with other men that may come to the valley and camp with the Cherokee, the red man. My mind wants that I speak other words— words of my thoughts—words of memory and youth."

"Is it so wrong to desire possession of things which seem to be so magical that they mystify one beyond the boundaries of common judgment? They cloud the mind with visions so that one fails to judge with wisdom. I find haste in the judgment of White Wolf. I have memories of young days. I was brave, daring and ruthless. There have been times when I made poor judgment. Many times I came face to face with death because of frail judgment. Those memories have no need of spoken words. Before Yellow Bear was two years old, another tribe raided ours and killed his mother. Many times Little Fox grieved for her; By the time Yellow Bear was old enough to travel with him he had lost all hope. Then one day grief had clouded his mind, his judgment; he is no more, so I am the guardian of Yellow Bear. He is my shadow. These medicine sticks were meant to be given as presents to Little Fox, one who should today be running through these valleys, free and happy like the Yellow Bear. Tonight they will be unrolled from the animal skin that has protected them since his death. Now they will be presented to one whose small age has not passed. Now, I wish to speak of those that have endured since their beginning in these mountains. These mountains that have been the home of the elk, bear and buffalo that made trails that wind from the cane bottoms with rife winter feed to green grass that is plentiful in summer. In the high blue mountains. The home of the wind – home of the mountain spirits that gave us language to speak – words of wisdom – traditions to follow. These spirits have no influence over medicine sticks that remain covered from the light of the morning sun. Tonight the sticks will be uncovered, once again to be held in the night air, to be carried from the pow wow under a yellow moon. My wish is that these medicine sticks be unrolled by our Chief and presented to one who is special this night."

He handed the animal skin roll to the Chief. He stood up and carefully unrolled the medicine sticks. There were four sticks, two large and two small. The larger ones were about ten inches long and about one inch round. The other two were about half that size. All four of them were most unbelievably polished from the unknown years of handling and were now yellowing from their years of darkness.

He spoke, "Yellow Bear, I speak to you with wonder. Will these medicine sticks burden your shoulders with ownership that some day you might become a wise man? Or will they be trampled in the dust under your feet as playthings of one that is young? That decision, only you can make. One who is wise spoke of you as having long ears that catch words. It is good that you have long ears that catch words. But you must have sharp eyes – eyes that ask questions of what they see. Someday you may sit on the council to judge another man. Do not judge with haste, but with wisdom and fairness. When you are led into battle, what your eyes see, what your ears hear must be judged with a swift mind. Yellow Bear, you have youth in your favor. You are fortunate. You have footsteps to follow – footsteps of one that is wise. Walk in them carefully for they will be difficult to follow. I present these medicine sticks to you and hope they might bring you wisdom so that you may speak other words that are wise, long before age permits you to sit at the council of wise men."

Black Raven knew that Yellow Bear would not speak or show any emotion at the council, but when he stood up to accept the roll of medicine sticks his cheeks were streaked with the tears of one who has a soft heart. That maked Black Raven very proud.

All of the next day Yellow Bear was anxious for the day to pass so he could listen in on the council. That night when the bargaining was finished, the Chief, the medicine men and the elders passed the peace pipe to the leader of the men in iron hats and his officers, then the trade was sealed. Tomorrow would be the exchange of items. Yellow Bear was real proud that he'd thought about making a little mine and wondering if his grandfather might give him one of the iron knives that was to be traded for the silver.

Yellow Bear hardly slept for thinking about the items the medicine men would trade for. He had seen many iron pots and knives. He guessed that he'd seen about a dozen muskets. The thunder sticks that could kill with ways of magic. He'd managed to touch one of the many furs with their black and white stripes. At the same time he got to glimpse one of the beautiful long knives they called a sword that was to be presented to the Chief at the place of exchange. The exchange, where will it take place? If he could learn where it will be held, he'd slip into a good vantage place and watch the exchange. He was up long before the first light of morning hoping to learn about the place of exchange so he could watch and listen without being seen. He followed close to the footsteps of the Chief in hopes he'd hear something. It was now sun up and all he'd heard spoken about was the little mine. He'd have to learn where the exchange would be before the Chief dispatched a messenger to the men in iron hats. If he was still in the camp, Black Raven would insists that Yellow Bear stay with the tribe and he'd miss watching the exchange. But if Black Raven couldn't find him he'd e free to stray through the forest. Yellow Bear was now more anxious because the sun was high in the autumn sky and soon Black Raven would find him. He'd much rather be out than in the confines of the tribe. He decided to go to the area of the false mine and wait, because he didn't have anything better to do.

Yellow Bear found a small clearing up on the ridge close enough that he could hear. He located a bush thick enough to conceal himself from view of the area. No sooner had he gotten comfortable than he saw two men that he recognized as officers of the men in iron hats. They came out of the false mine and looked around for about two minutes and then disappeared back into the darkness. A few minutes later they came out carrying White Wolf. Yellow Bear watched them carry him into the bushes and then hurriedly leave the area. His first thoughts were that he'd been hurt and they'd gone to get help, but why did they carry him into the bushes if they intended to help White Wolf? His mind began to run amuck. Why did they carry White Wolf into the bushes and then go away? Should not one be with White Wolf if he was hurt? He remembered Black Raven saying that these were strange men with strange ways. Do these white men not have strange ways and knowledge over many things? They will return; they must return to help White Wolf. When more than four hours had passed and still no one returned, Yellow Bear decided that the exchange had already taken place somewhere else. He knew the men in iron hats would come back soon. So he'd go stay with White Wolf until they returned. When he went into the bushes where they'd take White Wolf, he couldn't find him. He had been here because there was blood on the ground. Deciding to pick up the trail of blood and follow it, he soon overtook White Wolf. When White Wolf saw who it was, he told Yellow Bear that he was badly wounded and Yellow Bear must hurry and warn the tribe because the men in iron hats were marching on the tribe. By the time Yellow Bear arrived it was too late for him to warn anyone. The entire tribe had been laid to waste by the swords of the men in iron hats. He knew he would only endanger himself to go near the wigwams to learn if some still lived. Before he could do that, darkness would have to come. While he waited on darkness he'd return to White Wolf and help bind his wounds. When he stepped into the open, three horsemen saw Yellow Bear and charged towards him. The three of them were almost upon him before he knew what was happening. He'd run one way and then another but he wasn't fast enough to run away from the three horsemen. Impending doom flashed before his eyes as the horsemen closed in on Yellow Bear. But he must not give up to these savage men on savage beasts. *Run! Run!* Was all his mind could think. Then it occurred to him that he must find a place to run into where the horsemen could not follow. His eyes caught a thicket, a bramble of holly that laid a hundred yards away. He knew he could not out maneuver the horsemen because now more had joined them and his only chance was to make it to the holly thicket. His mind said *Run! Run! Run!* The thundering hooves were following him and the long knives were slashing at his flesh as he dived into the holly thicket. Scampering on his hands and knees, first one way then another, until the thundering hooves faded. He was right; the horsemen would not come onto the bramble of holly bushes. In here it was possible to outrun the men in iron hats. His judgment told him that he was half way through the thicket of holly bushes and to stop, at least long enough to catch his breath, and survey the damage that the holly bushes were doing to his buckskin clothing.

The holly thicket had taken it's toll on Yellow Bear, the knees were torn out of his clothing and the flesh was bloody from the scampering on a forest floor that was thick with holly leaves. Blood trickled down his hands and dropped from his fingers making bright red spots on the brown holly leaves. But now the only pounding he heard was that of his own heart. Totally exhausted he sat down and began to reflect on what had just happened. He knew he had no home to return to, no grandfather to tend his wounds or care for him. The numbness of his loss had no other way to expression and tears began to well up from deep inside. His confused mind had only questions. What had brought this wrath down on his tribe? What deed had been done that caused them to be cut down like he'd seen today? Was it over the false mine? Was it because of the tribes desire to deceive the men in iron hats that brought on such a savage revenge? Was it his fault? Was it not Yellow Bear that first spoke of a false mine? The "False Mine" reminded him of White Wolf. Had they left White Wolf for dead? He realized the answer must be yes. But if White Wolf was alive, he would now despise the name Yellow Bear because it was his words that led to the false mine. He knew that White Wolf was close to the false mine and likely they would find him and finish his life like the others. But maybe after dark he could find White Wolf and they could hide until his wounds healed. Yellow bear knew he would have to go alone because White Wolf would despise him because of his words. Those words began to eat at him. Because of the false mine, his tribe was now gone. Yet he knew he must find White Wolf and help him. But now he would sleep until the stars came out. He was so exhausted that he paid no mind to his bed of holly and drifted off to sleep. When he awoke the stars told him that the night was young and the air told him the chill of night was not far away. At first carefully listening, and then surveying his direction, he began to work his way towards the false mine to search for White Wolf.

When he got into the area where he'd left White Wolf he began to imitate the song of the night bird. Throughout the area he repeated the sound, over and over, only to hear no reply. Deciding that White Wolf was dead, he'd set his course to the north, far away. He located the north star and set a course that he'd follow until sun up. He knew to travel at a slow pace until he was safely out of range of the enemy, then it would be safe to travel by day. He heard of a friendly tribe that was somewhere in the north, about ten or fifteen days travel. Near sundown the next day he found himself at the base of a strange mountain with many cliffs and decided to spend the night. To ease the chill he'd break some thick pine limbs to cover himself with. He'd piled up ten or twelve limbs when he heard the call of the night bird. He returned the call and was delighted to hear the song of the whippoorwill followed by the call of the night bird. It was White Wolf; he was alive and not far away. He quickly located White Wolf and sat with him. White Wolf had many questions for Yellow Bear. He'd thought Yellow Bear to surely be dead. He knew one so young could not escape the long knives.

White Wolf seemed truly glad to see Yellow Bear alive.

Yellow Bear asked, "Do you not despise Yellow Bear?"

"Why do you ask foolish questions of White Wolf?"

"You are not at least ill at the Yellow Bear?" "No, I am not ill at Yellow Bear. I am much pleased to sit with him."

"Did the men in iron hats not take revenge because of false mine that I spoke of?"

White Wolf then knew why Yellow Bear was concerned. He said, "Yellow Bear I was the appointed messenger, I carried a message that told the place of exchange. The leading officer said that with my help they now had the mine that they wanted. He said I had done my task well, and now that they had the mine they no longer had any need of me, or anyone of the tribe. If I was to live I would only annoy them. In the dim light of the false mine his long knife missed its mark. He thought his sword had made its fatal wound. Yellow Bear, because of you, soon they will learn that they are the ones that were deceived.

The sun was up when Yellow Bear pushed his head out from under his cover of pine. His flesh was sore from the holly thicket. Today, every muscle in his body hurt and his heart was burdened. His emptiness told him he would soon need some food. His mind began to wonder from one thing to another. Thinking that he should be proud of his sage words, yet he felt no pride. Then he thought of White Wolf. Why wake him, he thought, and eased to his feet. His knees were so shaky he could hardly stand. Something to eat would help his hungry feeling. He decided to find a creek and spear some fish, but first he would make a fire. After gathering some choice dry wood, he took a sharp edged stone and scraped a handful or more of fine shavings and began to rub the two sticks together that would make fire. Today this chore seemed endless, but finally the shavings began to smolder and broke into flames. He piled enough wood onto the small flames to burn for about two hours. By then White Wolf should awaken and tend the fire until he returned. He began to search for something to form a spear out of. His favorite was the cane stick that grew along the small streams of the valley. He soon found a suitable shaft of sourwood and thought how foolish of the fish to go under the rocks.

This morning he was glad they did, because they made easy targets. Finding a suitable stone, he broke it to fashion a knife, then began to clean the trout. When he finished them he returned to the place of his fire. White Wolf was now sitting up, but he didn't look well. He must have feigned death real well to have fooled both officers of the men in iron hats, and that brought instant memory of yesterday. He then thought they are the ones that deceive; they are the ones to be despised. His thoughts of the false mine caused a smile to appear. It was a smile of satisfaction because of his words of a false mine, his sage words. If only Black Raven were here to teach him ways of revenge. He recalled his medicine sticks, his only treasures, were no doubt now gone. But maybe not, he had buried them in the floor of Black Raven's wigwam; his place to hide small things. No doubt by now they were only ashes, like the other wigwams. But maybe the strange men do not burn a village of wigwams. Then he wanted to return for his medicine sticks. But he would have to wait. He'd wait until the animals of the night had finished their work. Once Black Raven had spoken of these times - times of death- and how it is to be. His memory was clear. He'd asked Black Raven about the death of another tribe. Recollection of those words were clear; "Yellow Bear, they were the enemy. Sometimes we feast on the animals of darkness. The wolf and panther, they must be repaid. It saddens the heart, but tonight they feast."

Yellow Bear knew he must wait until the bones of his kin were scattered. Then, when summer returned to the valley of bears, and if the men in iron hats were gone he'd look for his medicine sticks.

White Wolf could see the worried look on Yellow Bear's face that only minutes ago wore a faint smile. He knew that a burden of worry was a false burden and spoke, "Yellow Bear, why the face of gloom? We live, we eat and by chance we set together. Is that not reason for joy?"

Yellow Bear then felt selfish, he'd not bothered to ask about White Wolf's wounds.

"Need I look at your wound and tend it with binding?" he asked.

"It is kind that you ask, but my wound is deep; it must heal from the inside. Yellow Bear, when it became obvious that none would survive I set out to this mountain of cliffs that I might rest and remain until my wound healed. Now that you bring me food and set with me for comfort, I feel that my wound will heal quickly. Then I will be proud to travel the distant valley with Yellow Bear"

A faint smile returned to Yellow Bear's face and grew large with pride that brought questions. "White Wolf, might you be my guardian and teach me, that I might learn ways of revenge?"

Yes Yellow Bear. Though I am lacking in the wisdom of Black Raven, I will teach what I can. Some I can teach while I heal. When I am well, you and I will travel to the lands of the Kipawaw, where powerful medicine men dwell. Where White Wolf has sat at their councils before…" recalling memories of the first time he had sat beside Black Raven. They had taken Yellow Bear's older sister there to be a ward of the Kipawaw because Black Raven could not care for both children of Little Fox. *Would not that be a surprise for Yellow Bear, but many years have passed and she might not be alive.* Knowing Yellow Bear would only be troubled by the knowledge, he continued, "Yellow Bear, I will be proud to return with sage words to their councils, words that favor one that is worthy of great learning."

"I have long ears, that hear well and with care they will listen to the sage words of White Wolf. Can we start soon?"

"Yellow Bear, your wounds may not be severe, yet they too must heal. Your clothing is not many days short of tatters. They must be repaired. Go to the place where the fish remains lay, and set a trap that will catch the raccoon. That tomorrow we may eat and have hide to repair your torn clothing When you return I will have words of you."

Yellow Bear hurried back to the place where he'd cleaned the fish. Using the remaining parts for bait he set two dead fall traps beside the creek and hurried back to hear the words of White Wolf.

"How many traps did the Yellow Bear make?" asked White Wolf.

"Two. Only two. Did you desire that I make more?"

"No it was my desire that you only make one."

"But, if one should fail…" there was the appearance of failure on Yellow Bears face.

"Are you disappointed that you did not ask first of my desires?", said White Wolf.

"Yes, I should have asked what you desire. I hurried that I might listen to your words and tomorrow have the answers."

"Yellow Bear, you need not hurry through life. It has many pitfalls and one should ask questions that he might avoid them. The men in iron hats hide theirs well, and cover them with smooth words like velvet that covers the antlers of a great buck deer. You must never fail."

"I have failed in ways that brought death and destruction down upon our tribe. It is truly sad that I survive."

"The Yellow Bear is not alone, because that you survive. Tonight I will speak to the Great Spirits and wish the White Wolf to sleep well so that he will heal fast and feel no sadness because of those who deceive. We will then go to the land of the Kipawaw and there I will learn ways to avenge our people."

Before Yellow Bear went to sleep he took some coals from one fire and made two, so that one would burn out leaving the ashes to prepare his raccoon skin. He was awake long before the first light and headed for the creek bank to check the traps. He had only caught one raccoon that was old. The other trap was still set and that puzzled him because the animals should be abundant. He returned to his place of fire and watched the sun slowly rise filling the darkness with morning light. That caused memories of Black Raven to return, reminding him of the times he'd awaken early and follow behind Black Raven when he'd go hunt for bear. It was this time of year when he'd followed too close and had been caught. Only one time had Black Raven scolded him and made him return to the tribe. There were many times when he'd followed behind that Black Raven should have scolded him. But now Yellow Bear realized that because he was fond of him he made no effort to stop his following behind. He felt sorrow that Black Raven's belongings were scattered about and not buried somewhere facing the morning sun.

He felt sadness and spoke, "Grandfather, Yellow Bear misses you. Now I have wishes, and hope they are not selfish ones. I wish that you speak with the spirits, to hurry the healing of White Wolf that I may follow in his footsteps to the distant land of the Kipawaw before the deep snow of winter comes." He knew that the cold of winter was not far and the skins of the bear and elk would be needed to keep out the chill from winter's ice. Soon the bear will hibernate and be most difficult to find. He realized that the raccoon were scarce. They had moved into the lowlands, and the birds of summer have gone away to their winter grounds where they could find food and survive. He would remain here with White Wolf. It seemed like the events at hand had all been set against him. He knew that tonight White Wolf would ask him to answer yesterday's words of teaching. He didn't have any words of wisdom to speak. White Wolf does not use words of teaching like Black Raven. White Wolf speaks words that say it is sad to survive, but also his words say we live, we eat; is that not reason for joy? He knew that he'd have no answers and would disappoint White wolf by asking for answers. Maybe he should think of things to entertain himself and set aside his concern about tomorrow. He stood up thinking of ways to pretend, like the old squaw had said he should do to stay from under her feet with his bothersome ways. He could not turn his mind away from common sense, but what would it hurt to ponder foolish thoughts. Thinking of his earliest days, memories returned of when he would play make believe with other children that had fathers. Because he had no father, he was chosen to make raids of make believe on their tribe. A smile began to grow because Black Raven had taught him how to distract them so that he could easily plunder their tribes possessions. They would soon tire and quit playing with him. The smile didn't last because that was only make believe, yet he could not erase his grandfather's words from the childish days.

"Yellow Bear, it is most foolish to enter a den of the bear in summertime. Yet it is most difficult to hide food from a sneaky badger."

Did those words have wisdom? Could he sneak into the tribe of men in iron hats and raid their supplies? There was no smile on Yellow Bear's face, only the blank look of despair.

"Why do you look so downtrodden?" White Wolf asked as he sat up.

"I have concerns about tomorrow, that when it comes, we might be prepared."

"Should we not first prepare the raccoon that will fill our stomach, that we might speak with more thought than that of our belly?"

Yellow Bear turned to look away from White wolf and spoke, "Is the panther with an empty stomach not the animal to reckon with…Does he bother to sneak up on the lair of the rabbit when his belly is full?"

White Wolf was befuddled by those words and said, "Is not that which is on hand to be dealt with first unless more graven matters arise? Does Yellow Bear desire concern without cause?"

"White Wolf, might it be possible to enter the tribe of men who wear iron hats and sneak away with their supplies?"

The words dazed White Wolf. It would be foolish to possess thoughts of entering a camp surrounded by guards that protect themselves with long knives of iron and muskets that thunder with magic that kills from a great distance. He must hear no more foolish words from the Yellow Bear. Then he began to have questions. *Has Yellow Bear been overwrought by disaster and now it affects his mind by…* The Yellow Bear has spoken wise words before.

He asked, "Does Yellow Bear have more words, more thoughts about what might not be clear to White Wolf?"

"White Wolf, would you not sleep well with knowledge that you had no enemies, no fear of anything no matter how great?"

"Yes, I would sleep sound throughout the night, but only because my guards protected me. Only the foolish are not prepared for the unforeseen. White Wolf has thoughts of regret that he'd not been prepared for the unforeseen. How wisely they had used words of velvet to deceive. Do you entertain thoughts of entering the camp of those who are strange?"

"When I ran into the holly thicket, I somehow knew that I must escape from the thundering hooves and savage men in iron hats. Now I desire to somehow find revenge and escape from them again and again."

"Has the Yellow Bear given any thought of how these desires might come to pass?"

"It is my desire to learn what White Wolf is willing to teach."

"Does the Yellow Bear have any knowledge of a skilled warrior?"

"No, but my grandfather was a great warrior. He said someday I would be too."

"Yellow Bear, I cannot furnish wisdom I do not have. The gift of knowledge, few men own, that it might be given away."

"If you speak what you know, my ears will hear."

"Yellow Bear, the men in iron hats ride the horse that affords them swift movement over vast areas", said White Wolf.

"How long do you think it will be befoe they discover that all they have is a false mine?" asked Yellow Bear.

"Yellow Bear, they could not be far from the truth."

"Do they realize that the real mine is not far? Might they mount a search soon?"

"Yellow Bear, you do fine sage words. It is wise that you speak of their search. They know the Yellow Bear survives. They will discover the White Wolf is gone and likely lives. When the search is mounted the Yellow Bear and White Wolf will be in grave danger of the thunder sticks."

"White Wolf, is it not possible that they may hunt for us as prized possessions?"

"Yellow Bear what could we possibly possess that they would prize?"

"Do we not overlook the real mine and fail to realize who now has knowledge of its location. Would not the life of one that has sole knowledge be spared? Were you not treated with respect, until you were of no use to them? Soon they will discover...Might they regret their haste and then search for one that still lives with knowledge they need?"

"Yellow Bear, your words form visions in my mind. For now I am more hindrance than help. Let's eat and sleep that I might heal and follow one with wisdom to the land of the Kipawaw."

They ate a portion of the roasted raccoon and Yellow Bear covered White Wolf with pine limbs. Then he crawled under his and drifted off to sleep. A vision of many horses feeding on grass with toadstools as their ladings lay scattered about in disarray, appeared in his dream.

As usual, Yellow Bear woke early. Today he would prepare the skin of the raccoon for his clothing. Removing the skin from the ashes he began the work of blending flesh into the ashes that would make it tough and durable, he wasn't pleased with the color, but he continued until the task was finished. He prepared the remaining parts that he and White Wolf would eat later. When it was light enough to travel, he went to check the other trap and found another raccoon that too was old. When he returned White Wolf was sitting beside the fire enjoying his morning meal. Today White Wolf looked much better, he wore a smile for Yellow Bear. Yellow Bear was glad to see improvement in White Wolf's recovery which told him that soon he would be able to travel. But today he had many questions for White Wolf. First, he would ask of his health. "The White Wolf smiles today. Is that not a good sign?" said Yellow Bear.

"Yes, it is a good sign. I am pleased; when I awoke there was no fresh blood from my wound."

"White Wolf, the spirits answer Yellow Bear. To them, what do I owe?"

"Yellow Bear, I am not fully healed, but when I am and the spirits of morning look down and see the smile of Yellow Bear, they will ask no payment."

By midday they had the second raccoon hide dressed and in the ashes curing so that in two more days they could repair the clothes of Yellow Bear. When three days passed they would begin their venture to the north.

Yellow Bear was not anxious to leave, but something was troubling him; a desire to go, but something was saying, stay. Did he really want to go away? No, but he must – only if his tribe was still – he could still vision the small village of wigwams, his home where he knew each member of the tribe. Now he must go away, to a tribe of unknown faces to learn new ways. But White Wolf had sat at their councils before, he would help Yellow Bear. Help Yellow Bear. Those words were of sour taste. Yellow Bear knew he must do for himself without help, but he was young and lacking in wisdom even in what he thought he knew. He thought he knew how to prepare the animal hides. Even with White Wolf's help, the hide was the color of dull black ashes. Even last night's dream was a foolish one. Who would be so foolish to let horses graze grass that had the poison toadstool??? The vision of ladings that lay scattered about. What meaning did it have? If horses ate the poison toadstools they would surely fall from under the weight of their ladings, they would fall with their ladings! White Wolf had spoken of the horses that move swiftly. Thoughts came to his mind; a smile appeared on his face. It would do White Wolf's wounds good to remain a few more days while he works. But he must work with haste, soon the men in iron hats will have all of the silver moved out of the false mine. Desires in his mind must be done with great haste. He would gather toadstools and mix them with pokeroot. The toadstool was difficult to find at this time of year, but he managed to locate a sufficient amount. The pokeroot was plentiful and he soon gathered what he needed. He would have to use the finished raccoon skin to carry the poisonous mixture. He hurried about drying the few toadstools and pokeroot so it would be ready by tomorrow night. Throughout the day White Wolf kept asking why he scurried about like the ground squirrel. Yellow Bear knew the wise keep their knowledge but he was tempted to speak about his intentions. The way White Wolf kept busy working with the ashes and raccoon skins, even he didn't like the color.

White Wolf noticed that Yellow Bear was not pleased with the raccoon skin and asked, "Is the color of darkness displeasing to Yellow Bear?"

"It is not the brown color it should be" said Yellow Bear.

"I have prepared more ashes which will color your clothing, the same color."

"Why would I wish to color my clothing?"

"Do you not desire to raid the camp of those who wear iron hats?"

"How do you know of my desires?" Yellow Bear asked in surprise. "I had no knowledge, until now. Did you not ask White Wolf for words of wisdom? Yellow Bear, one who has traveled in darkness, with fear as his sole companion knows the value of clothing that is dark as the night. The raccoon skin was purposely colored like the darkness. Tonight I will speak with the spirits of night, of my wish, that dust falling from your clothing will make more sound than your footsteps and that your eyes will see with vision of the owl. Now go to the high mountain that you may see into the valley camp of men in iron hats. Remain there and study for two days, study each movement of the tribe. Learn where the feed grain is kept. Watch with care where each guard is placed so that you may learn the safe place to enter from one side. Do what you must, then leave by the other side. Never return by the same path you enter. I am of the belief that they would never vision one so young to be brave enough to raid only one horse!"

"Take one horse!" said Yellow Bear.

"Is it not easier for White Wolf to ride to the land of the Kipawaw on a horse behind the Yellow Bear? It would be sad that each one should perish. I watched as men on horses run thundering across valley floor. I have asked the spirits to help guide you so that thundering hooves will cease to carry those who speak with a forked tongue. Yellow Bear, prepare your clothing and then go swiftly to the mountain tops that afford vision that will assure you a successful raid of the men in iron hats. Go with no concern for White Wolf. He will care for himself."

Yellow bear knew to do exactly like White Wolf spoke. He colored his clothes and before they were dry he took the poison and carefully worked his way up a long ridge to the high mountain crest where he could see the entire camp site of the men in iron hats and began his vigil that he would learn the lay of their camp. He watched as loaded horses came from the area of the false mine. They were in no hurry, he knew that was good and maybe they haven't yet cleaned the false mine of its contents. Yellow Bear noticed one that did not wear the armor of iron, but he must be one of command, he seemed to give instructions to one then another as he hurried about on a horse that was black as the raven, it was shiny as the crow's wing and he watched as the black horse pranced about with its rider. It was a spirited animal and maybe it should be the one to take. The more Yellow Bear watched, the more his heart desired the black one. He watched as the men would take the feed rations to each horse where they were tied and by sundown he'd located where the feed grain was kept. As far as he could tell, the feed stock was not guarded at all. The glossy black one was tied near a wigwam they called a tent. Those who appeared to be guards were loosely scattered about. Yellow Bear thought if the men in iron hats were convinced that they have no fear of the Indians, there would be no need for guards against anything more than the animals of darkness. He thought to himself that as long as the animals of darkness feast, the men in iron hats will have no concern for them either. He kept the vigil until the campfires died down and he could no longer see any movement in the camp. Then he crawled in under some low pine bushed and went to sleep. He must have been tired from yesterdays climb because he didn't awake until after daybreak. It did not concern him that he'd not eaten today. By tomorrow night he would know how his task would be carried out. This reminded him of when he would play make believe. But this was no make believe tribe he would raid. He thought of his words he'd spoken about the hungry panther, the powerful and cunning cat of the night that is truly a dangerous animal.

Throughout the second day he studied each movement of the men in iron hats, their patterns and habits. He thought, should I take the time to look for the bridle that will be needed to ride the horse or go without it, and make one later. He knew nothing about horses. He was not certain he knew how to lead one. It looked simple, he'd seen it done. And riding the beast looked to be easy. He began to wonder, *what would happen if the spirited black one scares easily?* Pawpaw fruit came to his mind. He was sure they were ripe, if he had some maybe that would keep the black one quiet and tempt him to follow. He knew where some could be found, but it was far away. If he went there to find that the animals had eaten them it would be in vain, but in order to gain wisdom some things must be done, so he would go to the patches where the pawpaw grows.

Running as if he was chased by some evil being Yellow Bear soon arrived at the pawpaw bushes to find that the deer and bear had been there, but it was not all in vain, some were left. Because the bushes were thin and spindly the bears hadn't managed to climb to the topmost parts of the bushes. He removed his shirt and picked what was left and ran back to his place of vantage. The pawpaws were ripe and the tempting odor reminded him of his emptiness, but it would wait, because each one was meant to tempt the black one and tonight when darkness would come he would raid the camp of those who speak with forked tongue.

He watched with care and observed the same movements as before. He continued to look for anything that might differ from what he already knew. Finally, the fires died down to glowing coals. When the stars told him the zenith of night had passed and now they slept well. Silently, he crept to the camp and entered at the widest points where no guards were. His heart began to pound. Now that he was inside, the camp was huge. From the distant mountain the eyes had failed to reveal its immense size. As he worked his way toward the center of the camp, his heart pounded furiously, what must he do first? The black one was closer than the feed stock. Knowing he must complete both tasks, the chill of night was causing he grass beneath his feet to turn white as he stood motionless trying to decide. He thought what if I go to the black one first, lay out some pawpaws within his reach, then go to the feed stock, lace it and the return for the horse. The frosted grass sounded under his feet as he stepped toward one of the small bushes that stood inside the camp. When he stepped under the limbs, his heart fell silent. The chill on his bare flesh was nothing to compare with the chill of fear as he saw his foot only inches away from a sleeping face. Momentarily he froze, then stepped over the man and continued toward the black horse. He raised his head and sent more chills through Yellow Bear, but the black horse made no sound when Yellow Bear held a pawpaw under his nose. As he took the ripe fruit from Yellow bear's hand, he thought this black one sure is big. He gave him two more pawpaws and placed two on the ground keeping the rest for later. He then crept to the feed stock and quickly mixed the poison in with the grain. He turned the raccoon skin to the clean side, stuffing the remaining pawpaws into it then tying it to his belt. He put his shirt on and crept back to the black horse and silently removed his bridle from a post where it hung. To his surprise it hung from an iron knife that was driven into the post. He gently pulled it out and stuck it in his belt. As he untied the rope with one hand, he placed one of the pawpaws to the horse's nose and gently pulled on the rope that tied him and he began to follow Yellow Bear. When they were about halfway to the forest he gave the black horse another pawpaw. As he stepped into the forest he gave the last to *his* horse. He was now free to run with *his* horse, behind him and he had a prized possession. He now owned one of the *iron knives*. He hurried to show White Wolf his black shiny horse that he raided from the tribe of men who wear iron hats.

He hurried through the forest to his place of fire. The sun was high as he led the big black horse up to White Wolf. The smile on Yellow Bear's face could not be described by mere words.

"Have you ridden him yet?" asked White Wolf.

"No, don't know how to ride horse. I'll watch you and learn how," said Yellow Bear

"You learn first. Don't know how to ride black beast," said White Wolf.

"Do you know how to put bridle on?" asked Yellow Bear.

"I watched it done when I was in their camp", said White Wolf.

"Show the Yellow Bear how. I learn fast."

White Wolf took the bridle from Yellow Bear and put the bits in his mouth, then pulled the rest over his head and buckled it tight. He then led him to a big rock and stopping beside it, he said, "Get on." Yellow Bear scampered up the rock and jumped on his back. White Wolf handed him the reins, saying, "When you want him to go left, pull rein left. To go right pull right. Pull both and he stops."

Yellow Bear thought, that's simple enough and he asked, "How do I get him to go?"

"Kick him in the ribs with your heels."

Two seconds later Yellow Bear was lying on the ground, flat on his back and the horse was gone. It had seemed to vanish, right from under him. He looked up to see a big black face looking at him. The black horse looked like he didn't know what happened either.

White wolf wore a puzzled look on his face, "Big black beast fast."

The shiny black horse came back and stopped, shaking his head beside Yellow Bear. Yellow Bear took the reins, leading him back to the big rock where he jumped on him again.

White Wolf said, "Hold tight to the reins, remember, pull both when you want him to stop"

Again Yellow Bear kicked him. As the big black horse jumped forward Yellow Bear pulled both reins – that sent him sailing over his head, only to land, flat on his back even harder than before.

As puzzled as ever, White Wolf said, "Stops fast, too!"

It took a few minutes for Yellow Bear to decide if it was wise to try again or not.

This time White Wolf led him back to the big rock and Yellow Bear eased on to the horses back.

White Wolf started to speak with more instructions. Yellow Bear stopped him.

"Me try it my way. You speak with forked tongue!" Yellow Bear had this idea and gently touched the horse's ribs with his heels. As he slowly stepped forward and Yellow Bear discovered the horse remained under him, his grimace slowly faded into a smile. He rode the horse part way around the mountain and came back to where White Wolf stood with a big grin on his face.

"You do good. When has horse eaten last?" asked White Wolf.

"He was fed before sundown, yesterday."

"Black beast must eat, soon."

"The Yellow Bear is hungry too."

"White Wolf gathered chestnuts, all day yesterday. Roasted some too."

Yellow Bear was hungry, but decided to feed the horse first. He asked, "Does horse like chestnuts? He likes pawpaws."

"White Wolf not sure about chestnuts, but I know that horses like wild clover. If this black beast is to carry us to the land of the Kipawaw he'll need clover. Roasted chestnuts you eat." he said as he walked away.

White Wolf had gathered chestnuts and heaped them in a pile for the horse.

How does White Wolf know of things before they happen? How did he know the Yellow Bear would return with a horse? Yellow Bear thought as he led the horse to the pile of chestnuts. He smelled them and began to paw at the pile until the thin husks broke open on some which he ate. Yellow Bear patted his black on the shoulder, and said, "You eat them, I'll have some that've been roasted."

White Wolf must have thought Yellow Bear would be hungry. It looked like he'd spent most of the day roasting chestnuts.

When White Wolf returned he had all of the wild clover he could carry and dropped it beside the pile of chestnuts. As soon as the clover hit the ground the horse was hungrily munching on it.

"Did you say he likes pawpaws? I found some."

"Where?" asked Yellow Bear.

"Along the creek bank, above where you caught the raccoon"

"I'll go fill my shirt" said Yellow Bear.

When Yellow Bear returned his shirt was full. Then he and White Wolf ate some and gave the horse the rest.

"The sooner we leave, the sooner we get to the Kipawaw" said White Wolf.

"We start for the land of the Kipawaw tomorrow?"

"First, we must repair your torn clothing."

White Wolf had fashioned a needle from one of the raccoon bones and with deft fingers he soon had both knees repaired. As he handed the clothing back to Yellow Bear, he asked, "Can I ride the beast and you lead him?"

"Two can ride on black horse. I've seen it done" said Yellow Bear.

"Are you not afraid he'll jump from under both of us?"

"Rub on ribs, he walks. Kick in ribs, he jumps."

"I'll hold feet…out!" said White Wolf.

"White Wolf, in what ways do the Kipawaw differ from ours?"

After a long pause he could not fully visualize all of the ways to answer Yellow Bear's questions. There were many things about the Kipawaw that he had fond memories of. Carefully thinking on that he said, "Yellow Bear, some of the old ones speak of distant places they visited when they were young. They can tell of distant sacred mountains and places where the lands are flat beyond the imagination. They describe great canyons that afford one to vision into the depths of the earth. I have heard them tell of uncommon trees they call cotton wood; and far to the north where cedar trees grow so tall, that only the arrow of the greatest archer can reach the top."

Remembering Yellow Bear's sister he said, "You can learn more. They have many talks where the old men sit with the young to speak their words of wisdom and age."

Again he wondered about Blue Dove, Yellow Bear's sister. Does she have the same name Red Cloud gave her? If she still lives, she is changing to a woman.

If White Wolf was sure she lived, he could speak about her to Yellow Bear, but that must wait until they arrive. *Is Dancing Bear still Chief?* He wondered to himself.

"Let's go to the land of the Kipawaw," White Wolf said.

Early the next morning White Wolf began to undress down to his loin cloth.

"Why do you undress?" asked Yellow Bear.

"Do you wish to travel with swiftness? We carry chestnuts with us that we travel farther by only gathering daily food for the black beast."

Yellow Bear then knew why White Wolf had gathered many chestnuts into a pile. He would use his garments to carry both the raw and roasted that would be eaten daily so between them the black horse could be well fed.

In no time White Wolf had the legs tied and filled with chestnuts, closing the waist with the tie string.

White Wolf was relieved when the black horse began to walk with its double burden. He knew if the horse humped from under him it would surely worsen his wound.

His mind slowly eased from the dread of a fall as they traveled along the base of the big mountain to the gap that would lead them north.

At the end of each day they would gather enough wild clover to feed the horse night and morning.

Each morning as his homeland had faded further and further into the distant blue mountains, Yellow Bear would speak to the spirits of morning. "Grandfather, I will one day return and avenge your death."

More days turned into a week, then two before familiar mountains appeared to White Wolf's view. Three more days found them entering the lands of friendly Indians where scouts discovered them and took them to the tribe where they were welcomed by Chief Dancing Bear.

Dancing Bear was marveled by the horse that Yellow Bear owned.

White Wolf hurriedly told Dancing Bear of the deceitful men in iron hats and how Yellow Bear came to own the horse.

After Dancing Bear inspected the magnificent beast he said, "Yellow Bear, this is a special beast. Its owner must have been of the highest command. It's bridle is made of silver, and your horse walks on silver shoes."

Jake leaned forward in his chair, chucking up the fire.

The wind outside was howling and snow was coming in through the cracks around the door. Jake got up, hesitated a moment then went to the door and opened it to look outside. "If this keeps up we'll be in here till spring." He said with a weary look on his face.

"Grandpaw, what do the Indians do when there is a blizzard like this?" John asked.

"Oh, I don't know, reckon they stay in their wigwams till it melts."

"What if they were on a hunting trip and got caught out in the mountains?" John asked.

"John, one time Yellow Bear did get caught out in a blizzard. He told about staying under a big pine tree for three weeks." I thought you'd want to hear more about Yellow Bear and his horse that wore silver shoes.

"Oh, I do, I do. Did the Kipawaw teach him the ways of revenge? After all he was just a ten-year old Indian boy against all of them men in iron hats."

"Oh, I guess he was twelve or maybe even sixteen before he learned the Kipawaw's way of illusion."

"Illusion, what's that?" asked John.

"John, illusion is a way of magic. Things can be made to change or move from one place to another if one knows how it's done." Realizing that John would just keep asking questions, he said, "Yellow Bear learned… Oh, it would be better if I went on with the story."

Jake began, "Dancing Bear was the Chief, Lord of all the Kipawaw, and he wanted to hear more about Yellow Bear; this mere child with courage of the warrior. Since no other from White Wolf's tribe had come to the Kipawaw, Dancing Bear assumed only the two had survived. It was customary to hold a council to hear word from other tribes. In two nights Dancing Bear would assemble the medicine men to hear White Wolf speak about what happened."

Two nights later:

"In the full dress of a great Chief, Dancing Bear stood giving permission for White Wolf to speak. White Wolf spoke slowly and with detail about the deeds of the men in iron hats, and how Yellow Bear's words had kept them from the real mine and his desire for revenge. When he was finished Dancing Bear stood, this time to speak his thoughts of White Wolf's words, but looking first at Yellow Bear."

"What are the ways of others that exist outside of these mountains? How little we know of these men?" He said musingly, "Had these deeds been done here, no doubt I would share Yellow Bear's desire for revenge, along with want of what had been bargained for." He said glancing across the entire group of medicine men. He continues, "White Wolf, a medicine man speaks that Yellow Bear possesses the courage of ten bears. Does youth hide the courage of ten bears? My eyes cannot vision the Yellow Bear being anything more than a hare among wolves." Abruptly he turned from the circle of medicine men, faced Yellow Bear and asked, "Do you know why I speak?" he hesitated.

Yellow Bear did not understand what seemed to be a riddle. Remembering what his grandfather had once done, he stood up and spoke, "Is it not wise to seek the answers one at a time to the riddle after the riddle is known?"

"Yellow Bear, had I finished, you would know I speak no riddle. Do you know why I speak?" Musing over the circle of medicine men he continued. "I speak with wonder about one so young. One that possesses desire to avenge and recover what is rightfully his. Is there

41

a medicine man here in this circle that is willing to teach this one, that I believe to be worthy?"

The oldest of the medicine men stood up. "Grey Eagle will teach him the ways of changing." He said.

"The ways of changing, is most difficult to achieve." Dancing Bear said as he looked at Yellow Bear.

Another one of the medicine men stood and questioned, "If Great Wolf is willing to teach the art of deception, how does one know the Yellow Bear is worthy?"

Pondering the words of Great Wolf, Dancing Bear asked, "Does the Great Wolf have anything in mind; a test for Yellow Bear?" Holding his hand up, signaling for no one else to speak, he continues, "The signs of twenty stones! Is that not a worthy test for Yellow bear?"

"Yes, the test of twenty stones is very good." Great Wolf said.

Dancing Bear stepped to the center of the medicine men, first to summon Great Wolf and then Yellow Bear. With a gleam in his eyes he said, "Yellow Bear, in two days, perhaps you will return to this council and describe how the test of twenty stones is accomplished." He turned to Great Wolf. His eyes growing distant as he spoke, "In two days, and Yellow Bear has learned the answer to the twenty stones, will he not be worthy of greater learning?"

Another medicine man stood for a moment, then stepped to the center facing Dancing Bear. He spoke, "Should he learn to answer the twenty stones, White Eyes will teach him more."

Yellow Bear turned to face the medicine man. In awe, he stared into his eyes and shivers rushed through out his being. Yellow Bear was staring into colorless eyes, the true sign of a great medicine man.

"Yellow Bear, you seem anxious to speak. Might you have a thought for some words?" White Eyes questioned.

"Words," said Yellow Bear, studying his three mentors, "I fear that if I fail the test at hand -my desires will be for naught." Fighting back the emotion that was fast forming into a lump in his throat, Yellow Bear urged, "Might the test begin, that I won't tarry in search of its answers."

"Yes, let's begin" Dancing Bear said.

Great Wolf reached into his satchel to retrieve the chosen objects. The twenty stones were made of pottery and were round, identical in size, about the size of a silver dollar. One side was smooth, on the other side were different symbols consisting of arrows - one, two, and three; a star, circle, square and triangle; a snake, sun, moon, heart, turtle, hand, fox, beetle, fish, buffalo, a cat and the last two; a deer and an eye. With the symbols showing he spoke to Yellow Bear. "Study the symbols, each one. When you are sure you know them I will turn them over, arranging them into a line. You will move four. I will move only one. I will tell you which symbol to choose. After you have a chosen stone, push it to me without turning it over. I will put it in my medicine pouch. When you have chosen four I will chose only one."

"You are able to tell me before it is done?" asked Yellow Bear.

"How else is one to learn? If you wish to start, push the fox out of the bunch so that I may put him in my pouch."

"Can I see the pouch?"

"Yes. Be assured it containes nothing."

Yellow Bear looked inside the pouch and handed it back to Great Wolf pushing one stone out of the line.

Great Wolf picked up the stone and placed it in the pouch. "Now, push out one arrow," he said with a demanding look on his face. Then it was the fish, followed by the star, the fourth one. "I will now push out the stone with two arrows" said Great Wolf. Then he placed the fifth stone in with the other four. Asking, "Now which stone did you push first?"

"The fox stone, one arrow, the fish and star. You chose the stone with two arrows," said Yellow Bear.

As Yellow Bear named each one, Great Wolf turned them over, in order exactly as Yellow Bear said.

The look of bewilderment on Yellow Bear's face was plain to see. Dancing Bear spoke, "In two days – In two days, we will again assemble for two reasons. One, for your answer." With a musing half smile he continued, "Perhaps you fail, in one. You may expect a pleasing surprise in the other."

Looking straight at Dancing Bear, Yellow Bear asked, "Is a riddle part of my task?"

"Yellow Bear, you must learn that Dancing Bear does not speak with riddles." He said as he waved his right hand at White Eyes and then walked away.

Suddenly Yellow Bear was more puzzled than ever. As he watched Dancing Bear walk away, White Eyes threw some gray colored dust up into the air. The entire circle of medicine men then vanished before his eyes.

With a feeling of awe, Yellow Bear stepped out of the empty circle of stones where only moments before some twenty medicine men had sat. Truly bewildered he walked to his host wigwam and crawled in under the warm pile of furs. Pondering what he had witnessed, he formed words in his mind. *Dancing Bear speaks in riddles, but they aren't riddles. I have moved the stones that change with a touch of the finger. I saw the lot of medicine men vanish before my eyes. Have I not stood among the powerful medicine men? Am I not in the land of the enchanted – Kipawaw; I must, with every ounce of my being, prove myself worthy. But how? How do they disappear as one stands among them? Yet, should I fail my task, I will be pleasingly surprised.* With a confused mind he drifted off to sleep.

He awoke early and fed the horse with silver shoes as usual, and then went about his assigned chores. He was working up to the point of asking White Wolf for some help.

When White Wolf became aware of Yellow Bear's intentions, he said, "Yellow Bear, I will furnish you no more than one riddle. If someone else provides the answer; How is the oaf wise from their words?" He then walked away. Yellow Bear rode the horse that wore silver shoes the length of the valley and back. Then day one came to an end and still he had no one shred of an idea how the twenty stones work.

Again he woke early. After the daily chores were finished, he thought of asking Great Wolf to perform with the twenty stones. But he knew nothing more could be gleaned from another trial.

He knew he had been given a test by one of the great medicine men. *Without the answer, how can I prove myself worthy?* he thought.

He recalled what Great Wolf had said; Push out the fox. Then he questioned himself, *How did I push out the right one?*

I must prove myself worthy. But how? He wondered as it was now nearing midday.

In exhaustion he was almost ready to surrender to failure when by mishap he said, "Did I push out the fox?" Then it occurred to him that Great Wolf had looked at each stone before he placed them in his medicine pouch. But what about the last stone? The fifth one. Great

Wolf had pushed it out of the bunch. He recalled something else that had been said, *Great Wolf is willing to teach the art of deception. Does the last stone deceive the first stone?* Thinking like this only makes more riddles, he decided. Yet White Wolf had said he would furnish him a riddle. How could his riddle help furnish the answer? Remembering White Wolf's riddle and shaking his unruly mop of hair, he said aloud, "If someone provides the answer, how is the oaf wise from their words? Might the oaf be wise to figure out how the medicine men vanish? Is the riddle part of the answer? Might the answer lie in a riddle?"

Befuddled, and knowing he could not answer the test, he gave up.

Somewhat anxious to learn about his pleasing surprise he took his place at the council. While awaiting the others, he decided that when Dancing Bear asked him to answer Great Wolf's test, he would ask him if the answer is in a riddle because he had no other idea.

Dancing Bear arrived with the most beautiful girl by his side that Yellow Bear had ever seen. She had pale blue eyes and carried herself with a most graceful manner as she presented a bundle of something to Dancing Bear. As he inspected the bundle he spoke to her with such a low voice that Yellow Bear could not hear his words. She smiled at Dancing Bear and remained standing at his side as he went about the ritual of assembly.

Yellow Bear now had a profound regret. A sorrowful feeling swept over him as he realized he must stand in front of such a beautiful being and announce his failure. Yet he must speak that he had failed his test.

Dancing Bear summoned him to stand and step forward. As he stood facing the great chief, the chief turned to the girl at his side motioning for her to speak. She held out the bundle for Yellow Bear. As he took the bundle and was looking into the fascinating blue eyes, she spoke with a voice of velvet. "Yellow Bear, I present you with a suit of garments."

It was customary for him to inspect his gift in view of his benefactors, but before he could unroll his gift, Dancing Bear spoke, "Yellow Bear go, change your garments, then return."

Yellow Bear was much relieved. Now, he would not have to speak of his failure in the presence of the blue eyed girl. *This is the pleasing surprise Dancing Bear spoke of.* He unfolded the bundle to discover some garments, and another surprise, a beautiful pair of boots made from the most supple deer skin. Who would care so much? It must have been White Wolf because he was the only one that would have gone to so much trouble. But the stitching did not favor his.

He changed into his new clothing and with a glow of pride on his face he hurriedly returned. The glow soon faded because the beautiful girl was still there talking with Dancing Bear and White Wolf. He stepped inside the circle of medicine men and turned so that each member could see his new clothing and kept turning until each one of the medicine men bowed his head in approval.

"Yellow Bear, it appears that you are well pleased with your garments." said Dancing Bear.

"Oh yes, very much, they are most beautiful. I have a desire that I may thank my benefactor."

"Yellow Bear, I believe Blue Dove has made your garments with no desire or want of words. May I present her, that you may be pleased. Yellow Bear, Blue Dove is your sister."

His spirit stirred at the words of the great chief. With exuberance of youth he beamed. "My sister... How could this be?"

"Yellow Bear, Blue Dove has been with us since the death of Little Fox, your father; Black Raven could not care for two. Blue Dove has been a most worthy ward of the Kipawaw. Knowledge of your sister has been kept here. It was desired by Black Raven. Had she not survived, knowledge would have only troubled you. Yellow Bear," he continued have you an answer for Great Wolf?"

Yellow Bear quickly reviewed his chosen words. "Does the last stone not deceive the first stone?" Before his words were finished, to his amazement, the entire circle of medicine men stood to acknowledge that he had correctly answered Great Wolf. He continued, "Yet, I fail to understand how the magic is performed."

Dancing Bear motioned for White Eyes and Great Wolf to come forward.

"Yellow Bear has not failed his task" he said. Looking first at White Eyes, then Great Wolf, he continued, "Is he not worthy of knowledge to work the twenty stones?"

Great Wolf laid out the twenty stones as before, asking, "Yellow Bear, do you remember the twenty signs?"

"I believe so," said Yellow Bear.

Great Wolf turned the twenty stones over and pushed them into a line, just like before. Then he said, "Yellow Bear, push out the fox." Yellow Bear pushed out a stone and Great Wolf turned it over. It was not the fox stone. It was the fish.

"Now push out the fish; he asked as he placed the first one in his pouch.

Yellow Bear pushed out another stone. It was the stone with three arrows.

"Now push out the three arrows," he asked and laced the second one in his pouch.

Yellow Bear pushed out another stone. It was the stone with the star.

"Now push out the star," he asked as he placed the third one in his pouch.

Yellow Bear pushed out another stone. It was the one bearing the eye.

Great Wolf placed the fourth one in his pouch. "Now I will push out the eye." He pushed out a stone to reveal that is was the fox. The he removed the stones from his pouch and laid them out with the fox in front. "Do you not have the correct stones?"

Yellow Bear had been right. The first stone does deceive the last stone.

"But Great Wolf, how did you know which stone to select?" asked Yellow Bear.

"The fox is thinner than the others," said Great Wolf. Pride shone on the face of Blue Dove. Her smile spoke of high regard for Yellow Bear, her brother.

Yellow Bear could hardly wait for the medicine men to be dismissed so that he could speak with Blue Dove, but when Dancing Bear asked White Eyes to perform for the benefit of Yellow Bear, he was in no hurry to leave the assembly.

Dancing Bear summoned for each one to return to his place in the circle leaving White Eyes standing alone in the center. He had with him a walking stick.

Yellow Bear could see it was carved with different signs or symbols on its entire length. White Eyes laid the stick at his side picking up a handful of dirt from the ground. He sifted it from one hand to the other until it was divided equally in both hands and threw it up into the air. Colorful sparks danced from his finger tips. A most colorful bird erupted from out of the midst of sparks changing into a velvet black crow and flew away.

White Eyes stooped to pick up his walking stick, but it was crawling away. A most fiendish appearing serpent was crawling from where his stick had lain moments before. White Eyes grasped the serpent by its tail. Speaking to the serpent, he said, "Stugil, did I give you permission to crawl away? You should know I would not permit you to crawl away in the presence of Yellow Bear." He held the serpent by its tail shaking it.

Yellow Bear watched it become rigid and change back into the walking stick.

White Eyes handed the walking stick to Yellow Bear. Just as he was about to take hold of it, it became serpent. White Eyes watched Yellow Bear cringe and withdraw his hand. "Stugil", he said, "You don't want Yellow Bear to hold you? You should know I have no use for a pliant walking stick. He bent it in its middle and kept bending and folding until finally he rolled it into a ball about the size of his fist. Holding the ball out, he said, "Go, find your brother." And threw the ball straight up. When it reached its zenith, the ball sparkled, bursting into a velvet black crow and it flew away in the same direction as the first one.

White Eyes bowed to Dancing Bear signaling the end of his performance. Before Dancing Bear dismissed the assembly, he summoned Yellow Bear, his guardian White Wolf and Blue Dove to the center. Yellow Bear knew he should have some words to show appreciation for the great wizard.

Facing Yellow Bear, Dancing Bear spoke, "Yellow Bear, has this council not pleased you by the wizardry of White Eyes, the garments by Blue Dove and the learning of, you have a sister?"

Looking up at Dancing Bear he spoke, "Great Chief of the Kipawaw, I fail to understand how my answering the twenty stones is worthy of the pleasures bestowed upon me this night."

Rarely was there a smile on the face of Dancing Bear, but the corner of his mouth showed the hint of a smile as he spoke, "Yellow Bear, Black Raven has taught you well. It is of my belief that one day you will, in your own right become a great medicine man. Youth affords you many years of learning. Though you have not been long among the Kipawaw, you have carried the weight of your tasks and chores well. Like the Blue Dove, you are most welcome to remain among the Kipawaw to learn the ways of White Eyes."

"About your desire to avenge? It is most difficult for the wisest warrior to walk two paths."

With the riddle, Dancing Bear dismissed the council of medicine men.

"Let's have a look at them taters, they must be done by now," said Jake.

As John dug out the potatoes, Jake poured two cups of hot spice wood tea.

"Well, where did Yellow Bear go to?" asked John. "Did he go back to the valley of bears to see if his medicine sticks were where he'd left 'em?"

John, most of the winter Yellow Bear could be found in the company of White Eyes and the horse with silver shoes. It was well cared for because every young brave in the tribe was helping to care for him so he'd get to ride the horse that wore silver shoes.

51

When flowers began to appear in the valleys of the Kipawaw, Yellow Bear knew that it would soon be time for his first test. He had no idea what Dancing Bear and his medicine men had in mind, but the medicine sticks had been mentioned by White Eyes, and Yellow Bear thought Dancing Bear might send him to see if they could be found.

This would be the beginning of many tests to teach Yellow Bear the arts of a medicine man. Dancing Bear had said that no doubt by now the men in iron hats had worked out all of the silver and were gone away. With this in mind Yellow Bear thought; *What is the reason to seek revenge?* The men in iron hats were in a hurry and by now they are back in their homeland with what silver Black Raven and the others had put in the cave. Now his main interest was to learn how to perform magic like the great medicine men.

Finally, the time was near. Dancing Bear would consult his medicine men tonight. Tomorrow, Yellow Bear would be sent away.

White Eyes had told Yellow Bear that if he returned with the medicine sticks he would teach him what magic they might possess.

That next morning each of the medicine men spoke to the spirits of morning, wished him well and sent him away. Yellow bear was very displeased; he had hoped to ride the horse with silver shoes to the valley of bears, his home place. But the test required that he go alone, and the medicine men would not even allow him to take his iron knife.

With only what he wore and one piece of flint he left. In order to put as much distance behind him as possible he set out at a steady trot. He knew that if he ate anything today it would be some wild vegetables.

Yellow Bear decided to travel for three days and then find a good place to make a camp because he would need a bow and arrow to take some small game while he was on the move. Thinking of roasted rabbit caused him to speed up his pace. Just before darkness fell he broke off several pine limbs, piled them up and crawled under them. Awakening long before day break, he had drank from a small stream and munched several mouthfuls of wild branch cress. As soon as it was light enough to travel he began his steady trot along the base of the long ridge that was familiar from the trip last fall.

After the fourth day he decided to stop at the next favorable place, make a camp and remain for a few days or long enough to make a bow and find some sprouts that would make suitable arrows for some of the young rabbits that were plentiful at this time of year. His diet of wild lettuce with an occasional mouthful of wild strawberries was fast turning him in favor of some roasted rabbit.

He came up on a large cedar tree that had been struck by lightning. The lightning bolt had splintered the tree into many long straight shafts of white wood that were split away from the light maroon colored heart wood. Thinking what a shame it's not hickory; that would be some very good material for a bow. He had never heard of a bow made from the white cedar. The white – outer wood was fine grained and looked like it would be suitable to make a bow. Picking up and bending one of the larger pieces of white cedar, he discovered that it was not well seasoned, but seemed to flex very good. With that he decided to stay in that area for a few days. He found a sheltering rock nearby and made a fire in front of it, and then he went about hunting for some suitable stones to scrape and shape the cedar wood into a bow.

He had crossed a creek not far back, so he made a spear from one of the long pieces of cedar, then went back to the creek and speared some fish that he cooked and ate. The sun was still high when he started working on the piece of white cedar that he hoped would make a good bow. Another week and he would have the bow finished. Deciding that some more fish and wild lettuce would make a good meal. Tomorrow, if he could find some strong vine in the area he would set two or three snare traps, perhaps he could have some tender rabbit for tomorrow night's meal.

Daylight found him spearing for some more fish. He'd went down stream to a deep hole where he'd speared a large trout and land it up on the creek bank. When he climbed up the bank to get the fish, he found the prints of horse shoes in the sandy creek bank. After a closer inspection he decided they were not very old, perhaps a week at the most. *Were the men in iron hats still here? If they were gone, who had made this fresh print? What if they have seen the smoke from his fire? Whoever is in the area could not have missed seeing it.* Another thought occurred. *What if there is more than one?* He knew not to trust anyone of them after what had happened to his tribe. Now what must he do? He'd like to stay in the area for awhile longer, but that might not be the wise thing to do. If something happened to him Dancing Bear and his medicine men would only know that he had failed his test. He must not fail this or any other test.

Might they have picked up his tracks and be following him? What if he left the area? He could work his way back to the land of the Kipawaw, but he was sent out on a test and if he returned with his medicine sticks, that would be proof of his trip to the valley of bears. If he finished the bow, that would be a good credit also. But would it be any good? He had too much time in it not to finish what was already started. Now he would have to move his camp and only burn a fire at night. But that would not be any good either because the keen nose of a tracker could easily locate a fire that was roasting any kind of meat. He must make up his mind, and soon. Perhaps it was only a lone hunter passing through the area that had made the prints of the horseshoes. So, he must go to the long valley and see if the men in iron hats were there. He went back to his shelter rock and got the cedar bow, sat down looking about for a moment, when Dancing Bear's words returned; "Yellow Bear, it is most difficult for a warrior to walk two paths."

Without further hesitation he knew that he must prepare the fish and then follow the tracks of the horse until dark. Tomorrow he would do the same until he learned which way they traveled. Thinking if the men in iron hats were still in the long valley, he could raid them again. After all it had not been difficult to raid them before and he sure could use one of the iron knives to finish the cedar bow. Another thought occurred; had they not fed the horses with the poisoned grain? Realizing the only way he'd answer that was to go to the long valley and see.

He ate the fish and went to the creek bank to pick up the tracks. By sundown he still had not learned which way the tracks went, they seemed to wander around in circles without any certain direction.

On the fourth day the tracks seemed to follow a southwest course along the crest of a big broken ridge. He tracked the horse along the ridge until it became too dark to see the ground. Four days later he was still following tracks that seemed to wander about in circles throughout the area like where he'd first picked them up when something caught his eye. It was a tall stick that seems peculiar. As he bent to pick up the stick a musket ball made its deadly whine barely missing Yellow Bear and tearing out chunks of trees and limbs along its path where his head had been a moment before. As the musket roar reached his ear he dived for cover of some thick bushes. Still clutching the stick in one hand and the cedar bow in the other he slowly stood up looking in the direction from where the sound had came. He knew the musket would have to be reloaded before it could roar again. But the man came charging through the thicket that separated them before the musket had fired. He had his long knife drawn, ready to finish whatever life his musket might have left. But his target had somehow vanished. How could that be? He had never missed anything at that range.

Yellow Bear watched him as he rummaged through the leaves for a sign of blood or anything to confirm that he had not missed the Indian boy. There was nothing. It appeared that the Indian boy had simply vanished in the smoke from his musket.

No more than ten yards apart, with only some bushes between them, they both stood motionless as one waited for the other to move. If the man moved in his direction, Yellow Bear was prepared to leap at the first step. Yellow Bear knew that in these thickets he could out run him.

Peering through the bushes, Yellow Bear could see that the man was noticeably shaken as he hurriedly returned in the direction from where he came. Then in a short time he heard the man ride away. When he was sure the man was far away, Yellow Bear drew in a deep breath. Realizing that he was still clutching the mysterious stick that had saved his life, carefully inspecting the stick, it wasn't much more than a twig, but something was very peculiar about it. Yellow Bear knew that it was some kind of shrub that did not grow in this area. It had been brought here from somewhere far away. Had the man used it to mark his trail? Were there more in his path behind him? Yellow Bear knew that if he continued to follow the man he would have to be most careful to avoid a second attempt on his life.

White Eyes had spoken to him about the musket, and how it would make a flash of light a moment before the lead ball reached its target. Yellow Bear had not seen anything before the cloud of smoke erupted from the musket. But, at that very moment he had been reaching for the peculiar stick. Again looking at this peculiar stick, he decided to keep it. As he tucked it in his belt it was obvious that he needed a pouch, an animal hide to carry things in, but that too would have to wait because he was more curious now than ever about the men in iron hats. The man that had fired at him did not wear the armor of iron but he carried a long knife like the men in iron hats. Now he knew it would not be safe to move around in the daylight. With this in mind he decided to stay here until dark and then set his course to the long valley, traveling only at night.

With the only piece of flint that he carried he began to scrape on the cedar bow in its middle where it would be held. He worked at this day after day, before sunrise and some more before sundown until it was finished, then he found the strong fiber vine that was used to make the bow string. The young straight maple sprouts were plentiful and soon he had four suitable arrows. He began to get bored with nothing to do during the daytime. He could sleep some, but it was days before he managed to sleep through the day. He continued this until he reached the area of the long valley. It was sometime after midnight as he peered over the dark walls of the long valley where low clouds hid the stars of night and shrouded the topmost parts of the mountain. When the first rays of warm morning sun had scattered the low clouds allowing him vision of the valley floor far below. Much to his surprise, the men in iron hats were still camped there and by mid day he had learned that some of the horses still lived. The amount was the total of his fingers on one hand and two of the other. Seven was all that he could see. Perhaps there were more horses that were outside the area, like the one he had followed. Yellow Bear carefully watched every move that went on in the camp, noting that there were no men or horses that could be seen moving around anywhere near the area of the false mine. Perhaps those that speak with a forked tongue were out searching for the real mine. Wondering about their disappointment, when they discovered it was only a false mine, brought a smile to his face and the memory of his medicine sticks that he'd buried in the floor of Black Raven's wigwam.

The valley of bears was only a short distance away; curiosity caused him to stand up and take in his surroundings. Today was a bright sunlit day. The air was hot with the beginning of summer and the trees were full bright green. Off to his left, he watched as some flies lazily buzzed about the carcass of a small animal. A fresh breeze from the North West carried a clean scent and caused the foliage to rustle in its wake across the ridge in front of him. Birds chirped throughout the forest that said everything was in order.

Staying on the back side of the ridge; - away from the camp of men in iron hats- he worked his way towards the valley of bears, and now the sun hung low as Yellow Bear stood silently looking over the blue-haze walls of the valley of bears – and ragged wigwams. The place he once knew as home. The men in iron hats had not burned the wigwams, but their long knives had slashed the buffalo hides of each one and long ragged-shaggy strips of the buffalo hides flapped lazily in the warm breeze. As he slowly worked his way down towards the valley of bears he knew it would not be safe to venture out from under the cover of forest until it was dark. When darkness fell, a few clouds drifted beneath a full moon that lit up the entire valley in front of him. It was a lifeless landscape, but somewhere a fire burned, the faint aroma of food told him someone was not far away. He hid the cedar bow and arrows in a small dry hollow log. Then slowly, he worked his way towards the wigwam that once had been his home. The animals of night had cleaned the valley floor, but a few bones of his tribe remained. As a dark cloud was about to slip from beneath the moon and light up the valley of bears, he stepped inside the wigwam that once was so familiar. The wigwam that once held Black Raven's medicine instruments and his assortment of roots and herbs that hung from every pole, they were now gone... All that was left was the slashed heavy buffalo hides that had kept him warm in the deep snow of winter and sheltered him from the fierce thunderstorms of summer time. The strong aroma he remembered was no more... *What can you do, Yellow Bear? Can you change who you are? Can you undo the wrong that has been done?* "No, but I shall have what is rightfully mine," he said aloud. Yellow Bear stood silently while a great satisfaction came upon him. He would raid the men in iron hats again and again until they have nothing left to keep them here. Tonight he must raid them. But first he would dig up his medicine sticks. He dug into the earth and uncovered the age old medicine sticks, unrolled the doe skin pouch that still protected them. As he reached inside a vision of that night when they had been given to him returned. Saying a silent prayer to the spirits of night, then hanging the pouch from his shoulder, the aroma of food drifting in the night air caused his stomach to roll. How many weeks had it been since he'd eaten a good meal? His diet of roots and wild vegetables was fast tiring. He needed some fresh roasted meats. The men in iron hats! No doubt they have dried meats. Closing his eyes to gain a mental picture of where the guards were stationed so he could learn the safe place to enter and leave their camp. As he stepped outside the ragged wigwam the low howl of a lone wolf startled him. His eyes then caught the bright red flash from the priming powder of a musket. An instant later its lead ball tore through the ragged wigwams. But before the echo of the musket had left the valley of bears, Yellow Bear was safe in the dark forest. The same man had missed him again, this time Yellow Bear had been warned by the wolf. But was it a wolf or had the man imitated the wolf thinking it would cause Yellow Bear to hesitate for a moment? If it had been daylight the advantage would not have favored the Yellow Bear.

He did not know that but the man had been tracking him for days. Since Yellow Bear had not been moving around during daylight the man had not been able to follow him very well, because he was always one day ahead of him.

There were no grey-black ashes to color his clothing and body. So mud would have to do. The first small stream he came to, he rolled over and over in it until he was covered with black mud. When the water had drained down from his hair, face, and buckskin shirt it made streaks that were lighter in color than the rest, appearing like some kind of dirty tree bark. By the time he arrived at the long valley where the men in iron hats were camped, his clothing was almost dry. Yellow Bear watched as dark clouds slowly moved above the valley, a single column of smoke arose like a strand of ragged cotton thread from the strange square wigwam; that was used to prepare the daily meals. He entered the camp unobserved and moved slowly through the camp. Shortly he came upon some muskets that were standing upright, one leaning against the other. He was tempted to take one. He quickly realized that if one was moved, the remaining number would fall in a clatter. On a post that was under the awning barely outside the doorway of a tent hung one of their belts with a pouch, a long and short iron knife. The many days of hunger had sharpened his sense of smell and because of his moving about in the darkness for the last four or five weeks his eye sight was like the owl. The strong aroma in the air told him he was near a food storage place. He would go there first, take what he could and then return for the belt with its knives and pouches. He located the store house, there must be more houses he thought, as he prowled around inside, because there was only a few pieces and strips of dried meat, and only one hind quarter of venison was all there was. He laid all of the venison strips across his shoulder, unhooked the quarter of venison and silently stepped out into the cool night air. Moving silently he returned for the belt and knives, and then made his way towards the dark forest. He couldn't wait to taste the dried meat and began chewing on one of the strips as he went deeper into the dark forest.

Yellow Bear did not know this but most all of the men were near the valley of bears because of the musket roar that was heard in that direction. The guards were awaiting word from their best tracker, he had been following the Indian boy for weeks and surely he now would bring word of the Indian's death.

Yellow Bear had eaten about half of one of the short strips of dried meat when he realized the strips were cut much thinner than the kind the Indian prepares

He thought, *the muskets would not clatter, if they were wrapped with strips of dried meat.* He laid the hind quarter down along with the belt and knives, rolled the dried strips into a bundle. With a renewed burst of energy he ran back to the edge of the forest and worked his way toward the standing muskets. In the distance he could hear some men talking, so he hurriedly wrapped the strips of meat around each musket and picked them up, cradling them in his arms. Slowly he moved back toward the dark forest. At the edge of the forest, about ten feet in front of Yellow Bear, a little to his left, a man stepped out from behind a large bush. He held something in his hand and pointed it at Yellow Bear. When he saw the red flash of powder, in that instant he knew to move. But at that close range the small caliber lead ball caught his left ear and tore out a rounded hole in it. Instinct told him to dive for the nearest cover. He bolted for the other side of the same bush the man had been hiding behind and vanished in the darkness.

"Grandpaw, Grandpaw Jake, how could Yellow Bear just disappear?"

"John, Yellow bear had always lived with death at his heels. He was only a boy in age, but in wisdom, well, even for one that young he had a gift for quick thinking and fast moving. Ever since Black Raven had taught him how to pull off them make believe raids. When he was only a child Black Raven had taught him to make decisions in half the time it took others, so his wit as quick, and so was his movement."

"When the high commander of the men in iron hats discovered that Yellow Bear had raided their store house of meat and took his belt and sword along with four muskets, well he really wanted to make life harsh for Yellow Bear. The men in iron hats wanted their muskets and the commander wanted his sword, and yellow Bear wanted the meat for himself. Yellow Bear knew that as soon as it was daylight the men in iron hats would be following him. So he had to put as much space between them as possible. He had a heavy load to carry, but he carried a real good supply of food, and some things were in his favor, he could travel at night and the men in iron hats could only follow his tracks in daylight. He was young and capable of enduring extreme hardship. He could travel at night and most of the day too, with only one two hours sleep each day."

"John, when their tracker reported to the commander, he described how he had first picked up on Yellow Bear. He told that he was on the far ridge when he'd first seen the smoke from Yellow Bear's camp fire, but when he back tracked to the area he discovered that Yellow

Bear was tracking him. So he set up a concealed position, only to fire his musket at nothing. He picked up Yellow Bear's tracks again, where he followed him to the valley of bears, only to fire at a shadow in the moon light. On that same night, the high commander himself had fired at Yellow Bear only to see a blur of movement that carried off four of his muskets. By now their tracker was of the opinion that he had been following some kind of phantom. Because of this, he had one of his men make silver bullets for him, and each one of the muskets was to be loaded with silver. Silver bullets would stop anything, phantom or mortal. From then on, the guards were doubled and instructed to fire at anything that moved in the night."

"Yellow Bear thought that he would be followed, but he was not, not by the men in iron hats."

"Grandpaw, who was following him? Did he go back to the valley of bears and get his bow and arrows? Couldn't he use them muskets against the men in iron hats?"

"John, by sun up on the third day Yellow bear had settled into a monotonous routine, one day blending into the next. He hardly noticed as the sun became a scorching red ball. He only paid attention to the northern mountains, watching them grow larger and closer. When he ascended a long ridge, its crest opening up a breathtaking view, where distant mountains were still snow covered. Only then did he hesitate long enough to inspect the pouch that he had raided. When he opened it he found it to contain lead balls and gun powder rolled in paper. Now good luck had smiled on him again. He closed the pouch, chewed off a chunk of dried meat and set out again without looking back. If he had waited long he would have learned that a large black panther was on his trail, following the scent of dried meat. But at the pace Yellow Bear traveled he was soon out of the big cats territory and the panther dropped back realizing that it was useless to try to take the good smelling meat away from something that never stopped and when he did, the cat could not smell the dried meat."

"Grandpaw, I've heard that a panther would jump on man or beast, if it was hungry."

"John, I reckon that old cat never had followed anything that moved like Yellow Bear did. You remember he slept under pine limbs, and it was early summer time, well when Yellow Bear was asleep, the old cat could not smell the dried meat because he had it in under the pine limbs with him."

"Grandpaw, I just thought, since Yellow Bear never stopped for nothing more than a little bit of sleep, he was still dirty from the mud he had wallowed in. I'd bet that old cat never had seen anything that looked like Yellow Bear did draped in dried meat, with a whole quarter of venison on one shoulder and four muskets on the other one."

"John, remember, he had his medicine sticks and the long knife with its belt hung across his shoulder too." Now if you'll quit asking questions I'll go on."

"No, Yellow Bear did not go back for the cedar bow and arrows. He had left it on purpose, remember, he had put it in a hollow log so it would still be in good shape when he returned and if he never returned well reckon he knew he'd not be needing it."

By this time the commander of men in iron hats was determined to locate the silver mine, because now he had learned that it was almost pure silver, much higher grade ore than his assayer had first reported it to be. Now he had to locate the mine. To leave without finding its location was out of the question and this one little Indian boy was not going to prevent that. Perhaps he would be demoted, maybe even lose all of his rank or life because he had blundered his mission.

By now Yellow Bear had presented his massive amount of plunder to Dancing Bear and the medicine men. The entire tribe of hunters, warriors and braves were impressed with White Wolf and his ward,

Yellow Bear, demonstrated how to fire the muskets. But now if the muskets continued to be of any use to them they would have to have a supply of gunpowder and the men in iron hats was the only known source.

At the second council after Yellow Bear's raid, some warriors wanted Dancing Bear to grant them permission to raid the men in iron hats, but when he discussed this with Yellow Bear, Yellow Bear spoke against it because the guards, no doubt were now on high alert. Perhaps in the dead of winter they might return and raid them without the danger of losing any braves. Yellow Bear agreed to lead twenty braves to the long valley, but only when he thought it would be safe, which irritated some of the elder warrior-braves. Dancing Bear came to his defense by asking if there was anyone that was willing to go alone and raid the men in iron hats in the long valley as the Yellow Bear had done.

Wandering Elk, the elder brave spoke, saying that if Dancing Bear would grant him leave, he'd raid the men in iron hats, there in the long valley; and he'd not be called Nashayeool: the brave with a hole in one ear.

White Eyes stood facing Wandering Elk and spoke, "Wandering Elk, you have courage, but you lack reason, or motive. Yellow Bear had reason and motive. He was sent to the valley of bears, that was his reason. His medicine sticks were his motive. Without motive, one is lacking perception and guidance from the spirits." Turning to Yellow Bear, he continued, "I spoke that I would teach you the magic of the medicine sticks. Perhaps our Chief, Lord of the Kipawaw, might like to see what magic that is held in them."

"Yes, I would," said Dancing Bear. "Would you bring them?"

Shortly, Yellow Bear returned and handed the medicine sticks to Dancing Bear, still rolled in the leather pouch, he spoke some word, chant words of a shaman, then handed the pouch to White Eyes, who unrolled the pouch, reached inside to find nothing in the pouch. He turned it upside down, shaking age old dust out of the pouch. In amazement, they all watched as the dust fell to the ground and began to flow like fox fire, then formed into some unknown kind of small furry animals that appeared almost human like and danced around the feet of White Eyes. "Where are your four sticks Yellow Bear?" he said with a deep hollow voice and handed the doe-skin pouch to Yellow Bear. When Yellow Bear took the pouch he could feel the medicine sticks still inside. As he opened the pouch the dancing animals faded, as dust would into the ground.

White Eyes said, "You have seen visions that are held by the medicine sticks. Now I will let them perform again, if you will permit me." Holding out his hand, Yellow Bear handed the pouch back to White Eyes. He took the medicine sticks out of the pouch, held two of them in one hand, lightly rattling them across the fingers of his other hand. Now listen carefully he said; and the entire circle of medicine men fell silent as the loud echo of a rattling sound returned from far away vibrating throughout the camp. Yellow Bear was truly amazed, the sound was made here, but it was heard, loud, coming from somewhere in the distance. Yellow Bear now realized that his medicine sticks held very powerful magic. Holding up his hand for permission to speak, Yellow Bear asked, "Do they hold onto wisdom?"

"Do they hold wisdom?" White Eyes said obviously not expecting such a question. He studied the two sticks that he held. Finally he said, "No, they hold no wisdom for White Eyes. Perhaps they do for Yellow Bear. Only with age does the shaman gain wisdom."

"Where does the shaman begin?" asked Yellow Bear.

White Eyes seemed very puzzled by the Yellow Bears questions. He looked at Dancing Bear, and asked, "Has the Yellow Bear earned the right to higher knowledge?"

"Does the Yellow Bear know how to read word-symbols of the shaman?" asked Dancing Bear.

"My grandfather, Black Raven taught me some. Perhaps my guardian, White Wolf could teach me more; I wish to learn the mysteries of life."

With a puzzled look Dancing Bear said, "Yellow Bear, the mysteries of life are not difficult to learn, perhaps it is only the rules of a game that you seek. For some it is easy to follow life's game. Tomorrow you can read the word-symbols of life's mysteries. White Eyes will lead you to the chamber of shamans word-symbols."

By noon the next day, White Eyes and Yellow Bear had climbed a ragged rock strewn ridge, up to a flat slab of rock that lay resting against the large sloping cliff that made up most of the mountain.

When Yellow Bear and White Eyes rolled the rock aside there was an opening to a large cavern. White Eyes lit the torch he carried and stepped inside the chamber. As he walked along the cavern walls, there was the writing he'd been taught by Black Raven and White Wolf. White Eyes held the torch high, he could see magical, symbol-words that described magic and words of wisdom. He carefully studied each word; each meaning of the symbol, but at the end of the chamber wall were symbols that were the same as those in front; but with a different pose. He went back to the front where the symbols began. He studied each one again, but more carefully this time. He could not understand the meaning of life. In the symbols that were formed at the end of the chamber wall it read: NO-WIN. THE FINAL GAME, NO ONE WILL WIN. That was what was written there, but how could that be? Then, from the depth of the cavern a light appeared out of nowhere. As it came closer a vision appeared out of the light. It was a shaman-chief. White Eyes quickly smothered his torch light, and now he could clearly see the head dress of an old shaman-chief shrouded in a glowing mist about him. Too startled to speak, Yellow Bear stood motionless as he studied the vision. When it moved closer, he tried to step back, but the cavern wall blocked his movement. The vision came to within arm's reach of Yellow Bear and grew brighter as words seemed to vibrate and echo from within the cavern walls. "Yellow Bear, your life is guarded by spirits of kinship. But you must play the game of life with fairness, then, watchful spirits will guide you until the final game-where you neither win, nor lose – you join with us."

John asked, "Grandpaw Jake, how old was Yellow Bear when he went back to the valley of bears? The long valley, were the men in iron hats still there?"

"John, Dancing Bear had chosen his son, Dancing Shadow to go with Yellow Bear to raid the men in iron hats, if they still were in the long valley. Then, at the next council of war, Dancing Shadow would be old enough to be elected lead warrior of his age group. If this raid was successful it would assure his promotion to the highest rank. Dancing Bear had planned for them to arrive at the long valley when the August moon was full. The August quarter moon would signal the beginning of their contest-games of autumn. All of the young braves and warriors were anxiously awaiting these games, had it not been for this festival, more young warriors would have wanted to follow along, and maybe it was because of this Dancing Bear thought it wise to send them to raid the men in iron hats. Perhaps he knew something else, but if he did he didn't tell Dancing Shadow or Yellow Bear."

"John, I reckon it took them three or four weeks to travel to the long valley. They discovered something that no Indian had ever seen. The men in iron hats had surrounded their entire camp with poles and logs set in the ground, with barely a crack between them, and only one way in and out, that was through a big gate that faced east towards the open grassy end of the ong valley. Now, it seemed that nothing could be done. It would be impossible to raid the men in iron hats, like Yellow Bear had done before. Dancing Shadow and Yellow Bear talked this over, deciding to stay in the area and watch the men in iron hats. If they had found the silver mine, Yellow Bear could easily learn if they were working it. Perhaps then, they just might kill off some of them as they made their way to or from the mine."

The next morning Yellow Bear and Dancing Shadow stood on a high ridge surveying the long valley when ten men under heavy guard marched away from the compound. They followed them to a deep ravine. Peering through heavy thick laurel bushes Yellow Bear watched as they began working in a dry creek bed. This was not the mine; it was nowhere close to the one that Yellow Bear had taken ore out of.

Puzzled at this display of labor, he soon understood why they worked in a creek bank. It was small pieces of yellow metal they labored after. "These are determined men that lust after shiny metal." said Yellow Bear. "Perhaps they will not carry out this yellow metal without some hindrance."

"But how?" asked Dancing Shadow. "You say they have many muskets when they learn that we are only two, won't they mount their horses and hunt us down?"

"The horse with silver shoes, I've been thinking about him; he should have a mate."

"Yes!" said Dancing Shadow. "Every living thing needs a mate."

"If we could raid two horses, then we could ride back to the land of the Kipawaw." said Yellow Bear

For a moment Dancing Shadow was pleased. "If we escape their muskets!" he said.

"I must do something to upset their plans without revealing ourselves." said Yellow Bear. "White Wolf taught me to study the men in iron hats, in order to learn about weak places in their defense. Now we can only spy on a few men that are outside. Those inside cannot be seen, we don't know what they do."

Dancing Shadow knew that his only purpose was to learn from Yellow Bear. Now, he had to speak. "Because of thirst and hunger, won't the beast be driven from its den? A few men must supply food and water for the others that are inside. Perhaps we could reduce their number, one by one, when they come out for food."

Yellow Bear knew that one or perhaps both of them may never return to the tribe of Dancing Bear.

When their observation of the fort was finished and nothing else could be seen in the long valley, there was no reason to stay there, so Yellow Bear turned and walked away. Following behind him, Dancing Shadow began to question Yellow Bear, "When will we return to the land of the Kipawaw?"

Thinking it a bit unusual that he had also been thinking those same thoughts he spoke. "You may return to the tribe Dancing Bear…I have no clan to return to. The valley of bears has nothing left."

Realizing that if he had no home to return to, Dancing Shadow began to better understand why Yellow Bear's anger was so great towards these men in iron hats. "Will we go to the valley of bears?" he asked.

After a long pause Yellow Bear spoke. "There is nothing left; it's all in ruins. The men in iron hats, with their long knives, they left nothing to be desired." Yellow Bear closed his eyes, and dream like he spoke again. "My cedar bow is not far from the valley of bears."

"A cedar bow? What kind of bow is that?" queried Dancing Shadow

"I was southwest of fox hill, about half way across I came upon a large cedar tree that had been stuck by lightning and some long straight pieces of white wood were splintered from it. I took one piece, as I worked my way to the long valley. I made a new bow. A white cedar bow."

As they piled pine limbs against a large tree, preparing a camp for the night, Dancing Shadow was thinking, *how is anyone going to get close enough to the men in iron hats to do them any harm? How can one deliver a deadly blow to those that were so well protected with armor of iron?* He realized this is a deadly game that Yellow Bear plays.

About fifty yards off to his left, his eye caught the movement of a heavy oak branch, perhaps a crow or large bird had just flown out of it, but there was no sound of wings and the tree branch didn't move like it should have if a bird had caused it. By now Yellow Bear too was aware that something was unusual. Without speaking, both of them blended into the forest to await something else to move. Perhaps it was one of the men in iron hats, if it was only one, maybe he would not return to his fortified encampment.

Dancing Shadow's mind puzzled as he stood motionless staring at Yellow Bear. Now, with an iron knife at his throat, his life flashed before him. In this moment, he now knew that he would never see the land of his people, but the man wielding the iron knife hesitated. This gave Dancing Shadow time to spring into action. With every ounce of his being he jumped, that should have thrown off any man. But with the vise like grip this man easily held him. The iron knife flashed out in front of his face. Just then Dancing Shadow heard Yellow Bear, in a tone that he'd never before heard.

"Tan Wolf, what are you doing here?"

Unshaken, there stood an old Kipawaw warrior, grinning. This man must be at least sixty years old, but he had the stamina and endurance of a warrior half his age.

He spoke with an old tribal dialect. "Dancing Bear send Tan Wolf to watch over Dancing Shadow and Yellow Bear." As he spoke, he took two more iron knives from his belt.

Seeing this display of three still bloody iron knives sent shivers running through Dancing Shadow. There had been three men in iron hats tracking them.

Holding all three iron knives in one hand, the old Kipawaw warrior spoke, "Three iron warriors, causem' no worry now."

"Yellow Bear quick, but no good." said Tan Wolf

Yellow Bear spoke, "If you so desired to test your skill of surprise on someone, why didn't you try your surprise attack on me instead of Dancing Shadow?"

"The Yellow Bear stands with tree at back-always. Dancing Bear want Tan Wolf to teach son lesson. Tan Wolf doesn't want to get hurt; I not need lesson; so I jumped on Dancing Shadow. Now, go back and bring up plunder."

Shortly Tan Wolf returned with two muskets, three long knives and the valued possession the "iron warriors" had carried Dancing Shadow and Tan Wolf was studying one of the long knives; it's handle was beautifully engraved, a fish like serpent covered one side, and what appeared to be an otter was on the other side. The other two long knives were just alike; each handle was plain hard wood of some kind.

"Just how close on us were these men in iron hats? We back tracked out trail many times." queried Yellow Bear sharply. "You have three long knives? The men in iron hats always travel in even numbers."

"Tan Wolf kill only three. Leave one alive, so he will go tell others how those warriors die in darkness. I think that might make cowards among warriors. Unn-they want to stay inside and grow more tales of dark night devils. Now, you guard area and watch Tan Wolf sleep like young pup?"

The next morning broke cold and grey. Al that morning a dull red sun shone through slow moving crimson clouds. About mid-day, Tan Wolf turned his ear to a soft wind that carried faint far-off sound of a morning dove. With a worried look he said, "Bad weather a coming this way."

"If we hurry," said Yellow Bear, "we can make it to a shelter rock; near the valley of bears."

Finally, when Yellow Bear stopped, it was for a moment to reminisce. Surveying the ragged mountain walls, once again he looked down at his home – his place of birth.

The old Kipawaw-warrior was studying the empty valley floor. Nowhere in all that valley, that Tan Wolf's eyes could see was there a sign of life – it was a dead land. As dark was fast approaching the valley of bears, Yellow Bear then pointed out where Black Raven's wigwam once stood, but there was no sign of it – it was all gone. Yet, a few poles of other wigwams remained standing. As twilight closed in the valley, wisps of grey fog that foretold tomorrow's rain, created an eeriness about the scene.

From his birth, Tan Wolf had been taught that to live one, must kill his foe. The very survival of one's tribe depended upon the skilled warrior. All of the Kipawaw had been raised up on such facts as these, but what kind of a man is this "iron clad warrior?" Nowhere had he heard of warriors that kill unnecessarily and unmercifully.

It was strange to Yellow Bear to hear the low growling sound-words made by Tan Wolf.

Unable to understand the old Indians dialect, Yellow Bear queried, "What is that you say?"

Finally he said, "Now, I know why Dancing Bear send Tan Wolf to help.

Led by Yellow Bear, nothing more was said as they worked their way down to the over-hanging rock that would shelter them from the oncoming rain.

Finally, two weeks passed, then once again the sun shone through a light blue sky to burn off the autumn morning fog. And now it was time to continue what they had come to do. Each one was aching to get away from the confines of the cramped space of the rock shelter.

Led by Yellow Bear they went to where his cedar bow was hidden. At first sight Tan Wolf knew that it was a fine bow and well seasoned. The bow was too strong for the string Yellow Bear had made, and it broke.

"Its limbs will have to be scraped down more," said Yellow Bear.

Tan Wolf asked, "Why not make a stronger string?"

"It's much too big to be of any use to us" Dancing Shadow said.

"It might be interesting to learn just how far it will send the arrow. It could be tempered with some wax of the honey bee," said Tan Wolf.

After gathering the material and making a new string, they took turns entertaining themselves, shooting the powerful cedar bow. Even Tan Wolf was amazed at Yellow Bear's accuracy with it, and remarked that he sure was glad that Yellow Bear didn't have it when he'd made the false attack on Dancing Shadow.

Changing the subject, Dancing Shadow asked, "How did you get the men in iron hats to separate far apart enough so you could attack one of them without the other shooting you?"

"You seen tree limb move, and that way Tan Wolf separate you and the Yellow Bear, that works on iron clad warriors too. Tan Wolf should be separating more iron warriors, right soon."

"We must start, somewhere," said Yellow Bear, "Where would be a good place?"

"Iron warriors stay one place, then go to get shiny metal. We pickum a place between"

At day break the next morning, they stood above the long valley, on the crest of a low ridge. As the sun rose, Tan Wolf's falcon gaze roved, searching near and far for sight of the iron clad warriors. His eyes failed to see any movement underneath the autumn forest.

"Soon-leaves come down," said Tan Wolf. Followed by more sound-words, that only he understood.

Finally he spoke, "Follow me and leave no tracks" Moving slowly down off the high mountain, he studied the smallest detail. No turned stone, no bent twig, no down- pressed blade of grass missed the old warrior's eyes. As they carefully moved off the mountain, Tan Wolf stopped many times, painstakingly winding long strands of spider web onto a small stick, then placing it in his pouch. No one questioned his actions, because they knew the web of the spider would satisfy some future need.

With the caution of a hungry devil cat, they crept along the forest floor. Throughout the day they would stop, stone like, and study a different area of the forest for any sign of iron clad warriors.

Morning would find them in a different area of the long valley. They worked their way closer and closer to an area that lay about halfway between the mine and fort of the "iron clad warriors."

Unknown to either Yellow Bear or Dancing Shadow, but as they slept the night before, Tan Wolf had placed so many spider webs across the big gate, even the amateur tracker could not help seeing them. If his knowledge of the iron warriors was right, they would soon be cautiously moving about.

Tan Wolf let his thoughts wander to things of the past. He thought about the way Yellow Bear's village had been laid to waste; and the way he killed the iron warriors as they slept knowing that would create fear and caution among all of them. He visioned the valley of bears; all the more this vision raged through his mind.

As evening was closing in, a mournful sound that could be made only by Tan Wolf, echoed throughout the long valley.

Tan Wolf wanted the iron clad warriors to know that he was stalking them. A squalid revengeful sullen savage was in their midst. He had no plan. He knew that when the enemy was close, instinct would guide him to do what he must do.

The cry brought two iron clad warriors up out of a creek bed in search of this ragged sound, as they stepped into the open area of knee-high grass. Tan Wolf stepped out of the forest and moved slowly toward them, as if he'd never seen them. Both iron warriors crouched, their heads barely above the grass. One of them readied his musket and waited. When Tan Wolf was about one hundred yards away, the iron warrior fired.

Yellow Bear cringed in disbelief as Tan Wolf crumpled, lifeless into the grass. Glancing first at the iron clad warriors, then at where Tan Wolf had fell, his mind raced, yet he stood motionless watching as the iron warrior that had not fired his musket dashed out, ready to finish any life that might be left.

Without caution, he arrived at the spot where Tan Wolf had fallen. He was gone. The iron warrior paled as he stood looking back, where only moments ago his companion had been standing, but he was gone. Now fear stricken, he held his musket ready with one hand – he drew his long knife with the other, and then shuddered. At that instant a flint-tipped arrow from Tan Wolf's hand and Yellow Bear's cedar bow caught him just above the left eye, ending his life.

The single musket report had every man in the area rushing to the place where two iron clad warriors just seemed to vanish. One iron clad warrior had caught a glimpse of where the fatal arrow had come from and fired his musket sending its silver ball crashing aimlessly into the forest.

As he hurried to reload his musket, Tan Wolf stopped in front of him screaming, it sounded more like a dreaded devil cat, a sound that would have terrified most any man. Terror stricken, the iron clad warrior froze in his tracks, knowing death was coming the next instant. Death did not come – but stark gruesome fear of the unknown raced through his mind. Finally, the iron warrior opened his eyes – the Indian was gone.

Yellow Bear knew that inevitable doom would come to more men tonight. Because Tan Wolf had taken a direct course towards the camp of the iron clad warriors, and was moving ever so slowly, through the shadows silently as if he were one of them.

Somehow, Yellow Bear knew that Tan Wolf would go to the far end of the valley, and work his way back. Crouched low, he moved through the darkness and soon was out in the open valley. Here he paused as the cry of a distant wolf drifted on night air. Perhaps it was his loved ones; lingering spirits from the valley of bears, or the spirits of his gods to whom he called. Night shadows moved with him.

Standing up to his full height, Yellow Bear withdrew three arrows from his quiver and placed them between his fingers as he moved into the darkness.

Remaining at the meeting place, Dancing Shadow turned his ear to a soft breeze. The night air carried a faint, far-off mournful wail. More sounds of the doomed drifted across the long valley. First one, then another and another. Occasionally, the night silence was broken by distant echoes of a musket. He knew that Tan Wolf and Yellow Bear must return soon – the rising autumn moon would bring light to the long valley.

The moon was still behind the distant, jagged mountains when Tan Wolf returned to the meeting place. He was half carrying, half dragging something rolled up in buffalo hide.

Yellow Bear soon arrived looking like a skeleton. He was carrying four or five muskets and long knives slung over his body in every way one could imagine. Not bothering to remove them, he fell in a clattering heap.

Tan Wolf's heart sank, and he knew something was wrong when Yellow Bear tried, but could not get up. After removing the muskets and long knives, Tan wolf discovered that Yellow Bear had been struck with a musket ball. His right side was soaked with blood from where the silver ball had torn out flesh, leaving a ragged-bleeding wound.

"We must bury plunder!" Tan Wolf cried. "Tonight, I take Yellow Bear to land of Kipawaw."

The tone in his voice indicated a most urgent need to leave the long valley.

Tan Wolf was hurriedly digging out a trench to bury their plunder. Puzzled by this, Dancing Shadow asked, "Why leave now?" It's a long way back to the Kipawaw.

Tan Wolf did not answer right away, moonlight shining down through open timber showed distress and sadness on his face. Finally he said, "I have failed Yellow Bear. Dancing Bear will be displeased with Tan Wolf." His words were deep and raspy.

"He will be displeased with me also." said Dancing Shadow. "I'll have no words to speak at council of war, or no plunder to show. We have both failed."

Throughout the area, where he'd buried the plunder, faint light of the moon shown through the trees enough so that Tan Wolf could see some stones that was near, and he dug into the earth under most of them.

Puzzled, dancing Shadow asked, "Why dig holes under the rocks?"

"When day light comes," said Tan Wolf, "Iron warriors, track blood to here. The smell of fresh earth will confuse nose of iron warriors, and he may not find where plunder be buried."

Dancing Shadow asked, "Why did you not bury the four muskets?"

"Lash them barrel to barrel, and use em' to make a litter so we can carry Yellow Bear, now must hurry. There will be nothing here when day comes!"

Perhaps Tan Wolf thought his actions might protect their plunder, never dreaming that others imagination could so easily be stirred.

The next day, thirty or more iron clad warriors reached the dense woods by following the trail of Yellow Bears blood; it looked like a whole tribe had been here, and had held some kind of ceremony at this one spot.

One imagined – the Indians went under some rocks – because they found no trail of blood beyond this one place. Another imagined, a whole tribe had vanished – into the ground, he knew they were devils, they had left overturned stones as evidence where they burrowed straight down.

Most of the men in iron hats were amazed by the fact the devils had all vanished, leaving no trail. One iron clad warrior knew that the young Indian was the same one he had fired at sometime before. He thought they would head for the high mountains, so he selected nine men to go with him to find and destroy the raiders.

That first time, he had found tracks of the Indian boy heading north. He'd followed them until a big cat had mysteriously came between them, covering the Indians trail, but now Yellow Bear had lost a lot of blood.

Tan Wolf had made a litter using the four muskets and buffalo hide. Then, as the zenith of night passed he packed sedge grass under and around Yellow Bear, hoping to stop the bleeding.

The second night found them moving Yellow Bear northeast along the sandy banks of the big river. Walking in and out of cane breaks, Tan Wolf had made his way to the front of a small herd of buffalo. If they could stay ahead of the buffalo, the moving herd would cover up any trail they might leave. If anyone was in front of them, Tan Wolf could easily pick up their trail in the damp-sand river bed.

Despite his tiredness Tan Wolf slept lightly during the day. Several times he awoke, to check on Yellow Bear, and found he was resting peacefully on the litter of buffalo hide.

A faint bird cry from across the river roused him from his one day time slumber. He was aware of anything that upset him would be bound to disturb the grazing buffalo When one grazed to within feet of where he dozed, he was reassured that for now all was well. Then, feeding near the river's edge, a buffalo shaking its head brought Tan Wolf's eyes roving the cane breaks. Perhaps he too had heard the haunting bird cry from across the river, yet the cry did seem unusual. Satisfied that it was nothing important, he smiled at the shaggy animal. Then studying the boy that barely hung on to life touched a part of Tan Wolf. He tucked the blanket of buffalo hide under Yellow Bear's chin and smoothed back a lock of jet black hair that had fallen across his face. Yellow Bear was not much more than a child that had so far survived behind an outward armor of determination and hatred. The disguise which he had worn for so long it had become second nature was an instinctive barrier set up against men that he had found to be such a cruel foe.

Tan Wolf hadn't noticed the cold. The wind was cutting, but here in the cane breaks it was sheltered, and the late autumn sunshine gave out little warmth.

"My stomach is empty and it's too cold to sit here and wait for one to die," said Dancing Shadow. "We live, and we should go back to our land."

"Our land," said Tan Wolf. Recalling the time when he first met Yellow Bear and his guardian White Wolf, the old sub medicine man; a past master of magic that had brought this lad to the land of the Kipawaw. Yellow Bear had been made welcome to the Kipawaw; and a ward of Dancing Bear.

Dancing Shadow was himself but a youth, and now likely would never be elected a leading warrior. Perhaps this was too much for him to accept, and maybe he resented the burden of carrying Yellow Bear back to the Kipawaw.

It returned to Tan Wolf the reason Dancing Bear had sent him on this mission, which reminded him of his fondest memories, and it made him gruff-inside-at least. Again he spoke aloud, "I remember how it used to be I cannot bring back one day of long ago – when I had to travel night and day." His voice trailed off, "Tomorrow night we must cross the big river."

The men in iron hats finally picked up the trail of two Indians carrying something, but by then, Tan Wolf and Dancing Shadow had carried Yellow Bear far into the north. Because they never found any sign of blood, many of the men in iron hats believed it was their muskets ad swords the two Indians carried off; so the iron warriors did not catch up to them. Tan Wolf was wiley enough to push on by night and by day until they reached the domain of Dancing Bear, where Yellow Bear was cared for by Blue Dove and White Wolf.

When the flowers were in full bloom in the land of the Kipawaw, Yellow Bear had fully recovered.

With an amazed look on his face, John asked. "Grandpaw are you making this up?"

Jake paused, not aware of the attention that John was paying to his story. Still staring into the embers of the fire place, finally Jake spoke…"John there is more to this story but now let's turn in."

With a jumble of thoughts running through his mind, John finally drifted off to sleep. He thought he'd just dozed off only moments ago, but now Jake was up and building up the fire. Seeing that John was awake, he asked, "John, how many eggs can you eat this morning?"

"Grandpaw, whats the weather like outside?"

"Well about thirty minutes ago it had stopped snowing." After a pause he continued, "when I brought in some firewood. Now, how many eggs do you want?"

Still John did no answer.

"John, are you okay?"

With a most peculiar look on his face he spoke. "Grandpaw I had a real strange dream."

"Okay" was Jakes reply. "I'm fixin' you four eggs. Then you can tell me about it."

Both Jake and John had washed and put away the pots and pans and John had carried in enough firewood to last all day.

"Now, John tell me about the dream you had." Jake asked.

Almost stuttering he started, "I_I_I, was-was, on this ridge overlooking a valley, I visioned a large panther. It attacked one of them men in iron hats. There were two of them. The panther had tore one in half before the other man shot and killed it." With a troubled look on his face he asked, "Grandpaw, do you know what that means?"

"No, John, I don't. Is there any more of the dream you remember?"

"No," said John, and remained silent.

"John, maybe I didn't mention this before, but when Yellow Bear was going back to the Kipawaw, that was when he had all of that meat, long knives and muskets. It was somewhere in the river bottom that he'd seen some really large panther tracks. After he'd left the river bottom and was high up on the long ridge, he heard the roar of a musket that came from somewhere not far below him."

"No Grandpaw, you hadn't told me that. Do you reckon a panther really killed one of them men in iron hats?"

"John, I'm sure your dream has some meaning to it. In your dream, when you seen the men in iron hats, were they on foot or on horses?"

Before Jake had finished, John replied, "On foot, on foot!"

Jake could tell the dream was troubling him so he decided to change the subject. Now the fire was really crackling. Casting shadows on the cabin walls. That reminded him of Dancing Shadow. Deciding to change the subject and not talk about his dreams anymore.

"John, I remember the tale of Dancing Shadow and how he earned a place among the warriors of the Kipawaw. You remember that Dancing Bear had sent Dancing Shadow to go with Yellow Bear to raid the men in iron hats."

"Yes, and he'd sent Tan wolf along behind to watch over them. Did he know that Yellow Bear was going to get hurt?"

"Oh, John, Dancing Bear could not care less about Yellow Bear. It was Dancing Shadow that was to earn a place of rank in the Kipawaw, because of Yellow Bear and the sage words that Tan Wolf spoke of him – powerful words of valor on the walk – away from – the long valley, that alone had earned Dancing Shadow a higher place of rank among the braves of the Kipawaw. He was now known as Dancing Shadow – brave with four feathers."

"Grandpaw, how did the Indians earn their place of rank in the tribe of Yellow Bear?"

After a long pause and still not answering John's question, he replied. "John, the tribe of the Kipawaw awarded the young boy, with his first act of bravery, one eagle feather. Then he was a young brave. From then on anything he did to help the tribe would earn him another feather. He could earn as many as five feathers. Then when he was seventeen he could begin to earn his breast armor of a warrior. John, the highest honor any one could attain was to wear the war bonnet – then he was called the Great Warrior – Chief of the Tribe."

"Grandpaw, you said that Dancing Bear did not care about Yellow Bear. Why was that?"

"Well John, in the ways of the Indian, the tribe came first. Had it not been for the horse that wore silver shoes, the muskets and long knives and the sage words of White Wolf, Yellow Bear would have been given only the worst of food and shelter of the Kipawaw."

"Grandpaw, you just mentioned sage words of White Wolf. What happened to him?"

"White Wolf, okay he was a sub member of the Kipawaw. An old medicine man without a tribe and White Wolf had been there before. I reckon I never told you about Yellow Bear's mother – the wife of Little Fox. She was from the Kipawaw. She had blue eyes; they called her Pale Blue because she had light colored skin. She had been thought of as sickly. Anyway, she was killed when Yellow Bear was only an infant. When Black Raven had no means to care for both Blue Dove and Yellow Bear, White Wolf was the youngest of the medicine men that knew the way of the land of the Kipawaw. Because of this, he had been chosen to take Blue Dove back to her people. Okay, you wanted to know what happened to White Wolf, because he was know by Dancing Bear, and had sat at their council before, he was made welcome to the tribe and allowed to share in the best food and shelter of the Kipawaw. He remained there for the rest of his life."

"Grandpaw, did Yellow Bear ever go back to the long valley and get another horse?"

"Yes, he went back to get another horse. There was nothing left. When he got to the long valley, they were all gone."

"They were all gone." With an air of excitement, John asked, "what happened?"

"John, I'm not sure what happened and no, I do not know where they had gone. All that was left in the long valley were some stubs of the poles that once had surrounded the encampment. It was burned and they were all gone, and the valley of bears, it too was empty. The only reason he'd went there was to get his medicine sticks."

"Grandpaw, did some other tribe of Indians do it?"

"No John, there were no bones, none anywhere. Some bones would have been left, had it been the Indian."

"Grandpaw, since White Wolf knew the way back to the Kipawaw, how did he know that. You said he was a young medicine man. Had he come to the valley of bears from the Kipawaw?"

After a long pause, Jake finally spoke, with an unusual tone in his voice. "John, you asked something I cannot answer." With that, Jake became noticeably withdrawn.

John could tell that Jake was in some deep thought. He had asked about the Indians and the valley's. It seemed like Jake always wanted to talk about Yellow Bear and his horse that wore silver shoes. "Perhaps I'm asking too many questions." With this, John decided to leave Jake alone with thoughts.

Jakes thoughts had drifted back to the days of long ago when Yellow Bear was a young lad, and White Wolf – White Wolf? Had he come from the Kipawaw to the valley of bears? That thought was quickly erased from his mind, never to be answered and replaced with his worst memory of all. If all of Yellow Bear's hatred was heaped up; He paused, hatred – hatred that was a word that Black Raven spoke to him about. He's told Yellow Bear of words that need not be spoken. They were about love and hate. Black Raven had said that love is shown by caring for the ones that are close to you and all things that you possess. Hatred – do what you can to erase hatred and "Never walk in the footsteps of one that harbors hate." Still there remained this vision that Yellow Bear could not erase. He'd paused to watch two children that were no more than five years old, playing make believe warriors, painting each other's face and body with the yellow mud – in the valley of bears – this same mud that had brought about his own name. He'd lingered there watching the two kids before continuing up the mountain side to watch the place of exchange. When he'd returned he saw the horror of what the men in iron hats had done to his tribe. Neither could he understand why and never could he erase what the men in iron hats had done to the kids covered in mud – the yellow mud – the crimson streaks across their lifeless bodies

"John, since it's quit snowing, maybe you should go back and let your mom and dad know you are alright, and when you are older I'll tell you more about the silver mines in the Unaka."

John stood up surveying the cabin when his gaze was caught by the calendar that hung beside Jakes doorway; he noted the date that he had circled. It was October 1843, along with some words known only to Jake.

John could sense that Jake wanted to be alone. He stopped in the doorway and said, "Grandpaw I'll be back soon and you can tell me about whatever happened to the horse that wore silver shoes."

About four weeks had passed before he'd told his dad about his unusual dream he'd had while he was at Jakes. "And part of it is most bothersome." He said.

"And what part was that?" asked his Dad.

"The man the panther tore in half, it-it- looked like Grandpaw, and that's the second dream I've had about him"

A pall fell over John's dad. "John – John I think you had better go check on your Grandpaw."

John returned with the worst of his dads fears, Jake Cooper was gone.

They took a work table out of the barn to Jake's cabin and had Jake laid out as best they could. John's dad asked him to straighten out Jakes hair because it was all matted together, saying "Son when these times come someone has these things that should be done. You are young and these are times you put away loved ones, there will be many. It is sad that he lived alone most of his life, he was alone. Go; tell your mom to give us her best blanket – she'll understand." John's dad could see that he was reluctant to go near Jakes body, deciding that John did not have to do anything if he chose not too. Then he walked out the door. As he closed it he said, "John, come on home when you get ready."

For the next week, John had been kept busy with the extra chores of caring for Jake's horses, chickens and the two pigs. John had even cleaned the cabin really well…

The two had been close, but all this extra time at Jake's cabin was bothering his dad. And he asked John, "Don't you think you are doing too much? I know Jake's animals need to be taken care of, but…"

"I've been working on something else too," was his reply then he walked away, again towards Jake's cabin.

The next morning John's dad decided to go see what else John has been working on. Near Jake's place he heard what sounded like someone hammering on a stone. Searching out where the sound came from, he found John working at Jake's grave. Working on his grave stone.

"What are you doing, son?"

Startled by his dad's appearance, he stood as if he didn't want him to see the stone. Yet, he knew his dad would at sometime see what he'd cut into Jake's grave stone anyway. "Dad, when I was alone with Grandpaw, you know, when you wanted me to straighten his hair, well I did, now I know why Grandpaw liked to talk about Yellow Bear and his horses that wore silver shoes."

"And what was that, son?"

John stepped aside to reveal a most perfect gravestone, and cut deep into the gravestone was Yellow Bear, and the date 1843.

"Why is this?" asked his dad.

With a broken voice, John spoke "Grandpaw, Grandpaw," then his voice trailed off. The lump in John's throat prevented him from continuing.

Puzzled by this his dad spoke, "John, you started to say something about your Grandpaw?" Then thinking perhaps he wanted to bear his sadness alone here at Jake's grave site. He turned to walk away, towards home.

With a barely audible voice, choking back the lump in his throat, John spoke, "Dad, Grandpaw's ear, it had a hole in it."

Recalling his Grandpaw telling about White Eyes, the great wizard, and word symbols written in cavern wall, he continues, "Yellow Bear-he stands among great warriors."

When John cleaned Jake's cabin, there, among Jake's possessions, he found the four medicine sticks, still rolled in the animal skin that held them together since time unknown, stirring the red mans blood that ran through his own body, but now time has worn away, erasing all the magic stories they once held, ancient stories of the medicine men, the shamen the old men that spoke sage words. Words that carried the wisdom of a story from one generation to the next. The magic of sage words that, that held the children spell bound…

Here ends the story of Yellow Bear and his horse that wore silver shoes.

Indian John; is this where his story began? You've heard one, the one he told, "If white man knew where it was he'd shoe his horses with silver."

EPILOGUE

The men in iron hats. They did record their quest for riches. But did they bother to record words of those who were here first? The tribe of Yellow Bear, the Scioto-mecca, those who were unfortunate, only because they stood in their way. Few written words are left, but maybe hidden away somewhere are sage words for those who are in search of answers, and White Eyes, a shaman of long ago.

Had he mastered the art of magic? Or has it too faded away, becoming buried deeper and deeper with each passing year, leaving no more than the imagination of the writer.

Buddy Johnson

Printed in the United States
By Bookmasters